The Lesser Of Two Evils

AMY PILKINGTON

Copyright © 2018 Amy Pilkington
All rights reserved. No portion of this book may be reproduced, distributed, or transmitted in any form or by any means without permission from the publisher, except as permitted by U.S. copyright law.

For permissions contact:
amypilkingtontn@gmail.com

This is a work of fiction. Names, characters, businesses, places, events, locales, and incidents are either the products of the author's imagination, used in a fictitious manner, or invented by fictitious characters running amok in their fictional world. Any resemblance to actual persons, living or dead, or actual events is purely coincidental, so don't get your knickers in a twist. If you believe you could be one of the fictional characters in this book, you might want to ask yourself why. This book is about monsters. If you believe you might be a monster, ask yourself why you identify as a monster. Anyone resembling such monsters needs professional help. Contact a licensed therapist immediately.

ISBN: 1718684282
ISBN-13: 978-1718684287

Library of Congress Control Number: 2018905463

Pilkington Publishing
Bolivar, TN 38008

DEDICATION

For Garry - thank you for putting me back together
and still loving me when I fall apart

ACKNOWLEDGMENTS

Special thanks to Trevor Galloway

A small ray of sunlight banishes the darkness and lights up your world in an instant. Everything can change in the blink of an eye. Sometimes those moments of sunshine, no matter how brief, are enough to carry you through whatever you must face in the future.

Prologue

My name is Laura Fisher Sullivan, and I am a domestic violence survivor. I was once Laura Bennett, but I fled a life no one should ever live. I was tortured and tormented by someone who pledged to care for me in sickness and in health, for better or worse, until we were parted by death. Fortunately, I escaped before fulfilling the death portion of this oath.

One in three women and one in four men are victims of domestic violence. Monsters are real, and they are living among us, disguised as humans and concealing their evil deeds and wicked ways from the rest of the world. This is my story. These are my monsters. It is up to you to decide who is the lesser of two evils.

CHAPTER ONE

I was born into a world of chaos, and my journey has been a trail of deceit, destruction, and misery. Still, I remain. I remain, and merely remaining is a remarkable feat.

My dad's illness prevented me from experiencing anything even remotely resembling a normal childhood. He was seriously ill before I was born, and his disease continued progressing throughout the next few years. Over time, his body developed a tolerance to his medication, and prescription painkillers failed to provide relief. When adding alcohol to intensify its effect no longer helped, desperation led him down a path to addiction. It began with marijuana and moved to harder and stronger drugs as he sought relief from his unrelenting pain. It was the only way he could cope, but it placed a heavy burden on the shoulders of a child still in elementary school.

A complete sampling of the most popular street drugs was hidden in our house at all times. Marijuana and cocaine were necessities to him as much as milk and bread were staples in other homes. Dad took a cocktail of various drugs mixed with alcohol most nights. He was generally unaware of his surroundings with little ability to move or respond. He was conscious, but he was oblivious to the world around him. It became normal, everyday life for us. This was our life, and we believed it was normal because it was all we had ever known. If you live with something long enough, no matter what it is, you begin thinking of it as normal. This was our normal.

Most of my childhood was spent taking care of dad and my sisters. As his pain levels spiked, so did his anger. His physical pain caused him to lash out the only way he knew how—physical abuse. Everyone around him was a target. His physical pain was simply too great, and he couldn't cope. I justified his behavior with this statement many times.

I took most of the abuse, allowing him to take out his frustrations on me rather than my sisters. One of my sisters had asthma, and I watched him choke her until she turned blue. After that, I did everything I could to protect them. Whenever they angered him, I intentionally did something worse to direct his attention toward me. I took his abuse so they didn't have to endure it. They remember dad as a good father because I diverted his attention from them and became his assigned punching bag. It was how I wanted things to be. I wanted them to be happy, and they were.

THE LESSER OF TWO EVILS

When I was in the third grade, my sisters and I stayed outside a crack house all night. Dad instructed us to wait in the car and keep the doors locked while he went in to speak to someone. I put my sisters in the back floorboard and covered them with jackets to keep them hidden. At sunrise, I was still sitting in the front seat watching and guarding them when dad finally returned to the car. I was my sisters' keeper, no matter the situation. This was just part of our normal. It was normal for us because it was how it had always been.

My childhood wasn't all bad. There were small bits of sunshine that made my life worthwhile. Dad allowed me to act as Santa for my sisters. I knew the joy of watching the excitement of small children on Christmas morning before I completed the fourth grade. It was the little things that made my life great. Those rays of sunlight carried me through each day, and I was grateful.

The last day of seventh grade, my normal was turned upside down. The electricity was turned off due to nonpayment, and dad realized it was only a matter of time before he would lose our house. My sisters and I didn't know about any of it. When we got off the bus, he was waiting in the car. He drove to my grandmother's house, and we ran to the porch swing, fighting over who would sit where. I noticed dad was removing bags from the trunk. He dumped our clothing in the carport and kicked us out without warning.

Dad stood in front of me and drew in a deep breath.

"You can't live with me anymore. Your mother will be here to pick you up in a few minutes." He paused and eyed each one of us. "Well, alright then."

Dad got back in the car and drove away, leaving us sitting on the porch swing in shock. None of us wanted this, but he had not given us a choice in the matter. Keeping up with his drug habit to deal with his pain was going to cost him his house, his children…everything. Still, he would not stop. He couldn't stop. His addictions had taken hold.

We started visiting him when he had electricity. Dad didn't pay the bill to restore power, but he found a way to keep the lights on in the house. He stole an electric meter off a barn and would go home late at night and pop it into the box. The meter was removed from the house and placed in the trunk of his car after the weekend was over, which kept the electric company from catching him for some time. This was our normal. We didn't know he was doing anything wrong until he was arrested many months later.

Dad made friends with a man who fled his religious family. Jedediah was in his mid-twenties and homeless, and he moved into the house not long after they met. I was puzzled by it, but I understood years later when my dad was arrested for identity theft and fraud. He stole his friend's information and used it to obtain lines of credit in various places. It supported his drug addiction.

His presence was beneficial to dad in more ways than one. Jed helped dad cope with daily life by keeping him company, providing a distraction from his pain, and helping with household chores. After a few months, we considered him part of the family. It was normal having him around the house while we were there.

My father loved music, and we spent much of our weekends singing and dancing. He had an electric guitar and would often play some of his favorite songs. When he didn't feel up to playing, he cranked up the stereo and we danced in the kitchen. After a couple of hours, dad was always in his usual state—a zombie slumped over in his rocking chair. This was our normal.

It was a warm summer night, and dad had a full supply of his favorite drugs. We danced for several hours before he began slurring his words. He would soon fall into the trance I knew too well. I turned off the stereo, sent my sisters to bed, and went to watch television until they fell asleep. I pushed a VHS tape into the VCR and plopped down in dad's recliner. Jed sat on the floor beside me. He didn't speak for a few minutes, and I was startled when he ran his hand up my calf.

"You are bee-you-ta-ful," he said.

I can still hear the exact way he sounded out the word. I turned off the television and went to my room, locking the door behind me.

There was a curio cabinet mounted on the wall outside my bedroom, and dad kept a small screwdriver on top of it. It was too high for me to reach, but I knew it was there. Dad used it as a key to unlock my door when I fled his abuse during drug-fueled rampages. After he unlocked the door a few times, I started wedging the furniture in my room between the door and the opposite wall. It kept him from opening the door and beating me. I would place my dresser against the door, my bed against the dresser, and my desk between the bed and the wall. Despite my size, I could move my furniture around the room in minutes. Speed was crucial to keep dad out, and I had plenty of practice.

On that night, I never thought to rearrange the furniture. Dad was out for the night, and I did not know this man knew about the hidden key that would magically unlock my door. All it took was a quick turn in the center of the knob. I didn't know he knew about it and didn't barricade my door.

There was a quick flash of light across the dark room as the door opened and closed. I could hear him fumbling in the dark and turning the lock on the knob. It all happened so fast, but I remember every little detail. I have tried forgetting, but the memories always return.

He covered my mouth with his hand when he reached the side of the bed. At the age of 11, I did not know what was happening, but I knew I should be afraid of whatever it was he intended to do. I could not escape. It wouldn't have mattered much if I could. Dad was too far gone, and my sisters were too little to help. All I could do was lie there, hoping he would go away without hurting me.

His hand ran across my thigh and pulled my underwear to the side. He struggled as I squirmed, but the intense pressure of his body pushing between my thighs caused me to fall limp. The searing pain of his penetration made me screech. He clamped his hand down harder, covering part of my nose.

I struggled to breathe, and it was a good thing. Focusing on breathing kept my mind from focusing on the pain. I became dizzy after a few minutes and didn't have the air to keep trying to scream. He loosened his grip on my face and continued his assault.

It was not a short encounter, and I feared it would never end. His movements were slow and purposeful. He took his time. Perhaps it was because I was unable to fight. All I was able to do was lie there and hope it would be over soon. With his full weight on my small frame, I still struggled to breathe. I blacked out, and I don't know if it was due to the pain or a lack of oxygen. It was likely a combination of both, but I am grateful I was not conscious the entire time.

When I regained consciousness, I saw light flash across the room as he left. I looked at the clock. 1:33 a.m. It was just a few minutes after 1 a.m. when I climbed into bed, and he was not far behind me. My assault had lasted almost thirty minutes.

I jumped out of bed and pushed the furniture around the room, barricading the door. I was frightened, in pain, and trying to understand what had just happened. Regardless of the responsibilities I had helping my ill father and caring for my sisters, I was still a child. I had not even had my first period. I looked like a child—devoid of breasts and pubic hair. What little semblance of childhood innocence I had left was taken from me that night.

I never hated anyone before that night. I had learned tolerance, forgiveness, and patience dealing with an addict. Anger was an emotion I knew well, but not hate. I learned it in an instant. Most of the hatred I felt at that moment was self-hatred. If I had been smart enough to try and sober up dad when the man rubbed my leg, it would not have happened. If I remembered the magic key and barricaded the door after he made me feel uncomfortable, it wouldn't have happened. If I had tried to run out of the room when I saw the door open, it wouldn't have happened. If I had bitten him, kicked him, or fought him before he climbed into my bed, it wouldn't have happened.

My 11-year-old brain decided I was to blame because I didn't try hard enough to escape or make him stop. I carried the shame and took the blame. I felt guilty and dirty.

Despite what happened, I never stopped visiting dad on the weekends. I was ashamed and too afraid to explain why I didn't want to go. If I made up an excuse, my sisters would continue going without me. It was my job to look after them. They had always been my responsibility, and I was determined to protect them.

I would sneak into their bedroom at night and sleep on the floor beside their bed, making sure they were safe. As horrible as it was, even then I knew I would endure it all over again if it meant they didn't have to experience it. I had taken many beatings in my short life to save them from the pain. I never thought twice about sacrificing myself to protect them.

As hard as it may be for others to understand, I was my sisters' keeper. Even at a very young age, I would have walked through fire to keep them safe. I had been taught they were my responsibility, and I did whatever I felt was needed to protect them, even when it meant putting myself in harm's way. A therapist once called it selfless. I called it necessary, and it was normal.

I had yet to learn this would not be the worst thing I would endure in my life. There was far worse in store for me. One event sparked a chain of events. It led to the bet. The bet led to a world of trouble far worse than I could have imagined.

CHAPTER TWO

After bouncing back and forth between houses, I finally landed at my grandmother's home. Life was far less complicated, but only for a short time. I enjoyed it while it lasted. It didn't last long. It never did.

I was the last virgin in my circle of friends. The thought of willingly having sex turned my stomach after what I had been through as a child. When I accepted I would eventually want to have sex, I knew it could not be something casual. It would have to be with someone I loved and trusted completely. He would need to be patient and understanding. That ruled out every guy I ever encountered, so I remained a virgin. Somehow, I became the Holy Grail—the last virgin. That is how the bet came to be. A group of guys bet on who would take my virginity. Each one hoped to gain those bragging rights.

Saying I was popular with boys would be a gross understatement, but I had no idea why. I generally didn't date anyone long because I dumped a guy the minute he started pressuring me. I did not have a choice the first time, and it was going to be my choice when it happened again. No boy was going to pressure me or talk me into it. The decision was mine.

Dad was in and out of my grandparents' home, and eventually, he was there all the time. My grandparents were older and had health issues of their own. They were unable to take care of him, so, again, I did. I stayed with him in the hospital when I wasn't in school, and I babysat him when he partied too much. That was pretty much every weekend.

"Grandpa, dad is in the laundry room pulling the washing machine away from the wall. He has a screwdriver."

My grandfather shook his head as he got out of his chair to stop him before he dismantled an appliance. Dad had moved from the laundry room and was standing in the bathtub, moving the screwdriver toward the window. My grandfather stood in the doorway with his arms crossed.

"Son, what do you think you're doing?"

"I was gonna feed these hogs some grass."

"I think it's time to go to bed and not worry about hogs."

Dad climbed out of the tub and handed over the screwdriver as he walked through the bathroom door. My grandfather and I looked at each other. It would be a long night. He shook his head and whispered, "I'm going to bed. Wake me up if he gets too bad."

I was used to it. My grandparents were elderly and

couldn't deal with him around the clock. They were unable to chase after an adult who acted like a toddler. I was young and much faster. It was easier for me to keep up with a man hyped up on cocaine and running circles around the house until he eventually crashed.

My job was simple. I had to make sure he didn't overdose again, didn't hurt himself, didn't steal the car, and didn't break anything in the house. If dad got too far out of hand, I would wake up my grandpa. My grandfather was a man of few words. When he spoke, everyone paid attention. If he gave you an order, you followed without question or hesitation. Most nights all it took was a threat of waking up my grandfather to get him to calm down and behave.

After dad's benders, it was always quiet the next morning. My grandfather would question me. "Everything go okay last night?"

"Yeah. Everything's in one piece."

That would be the end of it. Dad would sleep late, and the three of us would get everything taken care of around the house. This was our normal. It was much like my original normal, but with some adult support and without my sisters.

School was a brief vacation from his antics. The distraction was welcome, and I took very little serious while I was there. It was my time to relax. I dated a lot and ditched them all within a short period of time. The more I ditched, the more appeared. With everything going on in my life, I really did not have time to worry about serious dating. Dumping a guy was easy. They didn't care about me, and I didn't care about them. Their intentions were clear, and I had no interest. It was merely a distraction from everything I was dealing with at home, and it was becoming more than I could bear.

A person can only act strong for so long before they start to break. I was crumbling, and it wasn't long before my life spiraled out of control. Dealing with dad's overdoses and missing my sisters had taken its toll. I was depressed and started cutting my arms with a razor blade. I wore a bandana tied around one wrist and wore several watches on the other. It kept the cuts hidden, and only a few people knew what was beneath the odd mix of accessories. I really didn't know how to deal with everything anymore. The pain of cutting reminded me I was alive, and it provided an outlet for my frustrations.

I always had many responsibilities, so this wasn't new. I didn't know why it suddenly bothered me, and I didn't know how to fix it. It felt as if the walls were closing in on me. My grandmother noticed I was becoming anxious and started feeding me Valium right after I started my first job at 14. It didn't take long to realize it numbed everything. I became addicted and soon spent every dime I made buying them from another family member. After a few months, I was taking up to six before bed some nights. I took four caffeine pills every morning to get ready for school, and I usually ended up needing one or two more around lunch. I had become what I said I would never be—an addict.

At 14 years old, I had already endured years of hearing people say I would never be anything more than trash because I was a junkie's daughter. At that moment, I agreed with them. I was nothing. A nobody. Trouble. When I stopped to think about my life, it looked like an experiment to see how much a person could take before they broke. I had reached that point. I was damaged goods, and I wasn't strong enough to deal with life without drugs.

There were plenty of nights when I swallowed those pills hoping I wouldn't wake up in the morning. I wanted to have enough courage to press down harder when I dragged the razor blade across my wrist. I couldn't even do that right because I was a weak, useless waste of space. That's exactly how I felt, but I learned adding in extra pills helped chase away the fear and was almost brave enough to do it. I was getting there, and I was happy about it. At such a young age, I wanted it all to end.

My life was saved by two good friends. One friend knew about the cutting. Jack loaned me his watch to help cover up new cuts, but he spent a lot of time talking to me and helping me cope. He was the reason I stopped cutting. Jack never told me to stop. He helped me decide to stop and kept me from having the urge to do it again. I never had anyone tell me I was a good person or praise anything I had done besides taking care of my dad or sisters. Jack made me feel like I had a purpose, even if I did not yet know what it was. He made me feel like I had to be patient and find my purpose. Jack saved my life many times over the next few years. He never knew it, but he did.

Another friend found out about my addiction. We were close friends, and it rightfully bothered him as soon as he discovered the secret I was hiding. He snatched a handful of uppers from my hand one day and downed all of them. It upset me because I knew how bad addiction was. I had lived around it all my life and was dealing with my own addiction at the time. I told him I didn't want him tangled up in that mess. He said something that stunned me. "How do you think I feel watching you?"

I knew how it felt because I watched my father all my life. It didn't matter to me if I hurt myself, but I couldn't hurt someone else. Before that moment, I thought my actions wouldn't hurt anyone but me. Not once had I considered it could cause others pain. That was not who I was. I was the one who took care of everyone, placing others' needs above my own. I stopped immediately. It was a rough couple of weeks, but I managed and felt much better once I beat it. It felt like I accomplished something big, and it was enough to keep me going. The victory proved to me I was stronger than I thought. It was another small ray of sunshine.

I had really good friends. They all saved me at various points. My cousin kept me sane by teaching me a little bit of insanity was healthy. Vickie taught me a lot about life and just being free and having fun. She was a lot wiser than I ever was. I should have listened to her. My life would have turned out much different if I had heeded her advice.

A guy who recently moved to our town started hanging out with my friends and was soon trying to talk to me. He was nice—a decent guy. He seemed to have no interest in anything other than my time, and I was happy with that. The past was painful for him, too. His girlfriend was murdered a few months before he moved, and it was a big reason why he relocated. We became closer, and he started talking about the future. His ideas started including me, and no one had ever talked about having a real future with me. I was happy with the way things were going between us and started thinking there was something real there.

Despite the way things were going, we didn't go

out together after school. I usually did things with my friends on the weekends. My grandparents let me go anywhere I wanted as long as dad went, and he didn't mind hanging out with my friends. He'd drink. I'd drive. I suppose they figured I couldn't get in too much trouble while I chased dad around and kept him out of trouble.

It was then I met Peter Bennett. We were together with a group of friends outside a local coffee shop. I was sitting on the hood of my grandmother's car talking to different people I knew when he walked up and joined the conversation. He had bright red hair and was dressed in tight jeans and a black button-up shirt. I didn't think much of him. Peter definitely wasn't my type, and I was in a relationship and had no interest in anyone else. He tried getting my phone number before I left, but I told him I was seeing someone and that was that. Our meeting was insignificant, and I thought nothing else of it, or him, after that night.

My boyfriend and I dated more than six months before we went on an actual date. It was my first real date. Our relationship was pretty serious by high school standards, and there was definitely a connection between us. Just a few months before I turned 16, I lost my virginity. It wasn't planned and wasn't something we discussed. It just happened. The event wasn't traumatizing. The entire thing seemed completely natural, and I was quite relieved it was over. I was relieved it wasn't a huge ordeal, and it eased many of my fears about sex. My relief didn't last long.

Less than a week later, my boyfriend told me he felt he had betrayed his murdered girlfriend and couldn't be with me anymore. I was angry. It didn't take six months to feel like he wasn't ready for a relationship. It was an excuse—and a lame one, at that. No matter what his reason was, I felt used and discarded. How could I have been so stupid?

The breakup was a huge deal to me. I had given up something I held sacred and was kicking myself for being so stupid. When I left school that day, the first phone call I received was from Peter. I was a bit annoyed when he asked if I was still seeing someone. I had a feeling he already knew I wasn't and had been waiting for this to happen.

I'm not sure why I confided in Peter. Maybe it was because I hadn't had the chance to talk about it with anyone else. Whatever the reason, I told him everything. He was still a stranger, but I vented to him about feeling used. I was angry at myself for falling for a guy's games. After I stopped talking, he asked if I wanted to hang out soon. I told him I didn't. I had no interest in hanging out with him or any other guy. I had only been single a few hours, and it wasn't just some guy I dated for a week. It was a big deal to me. Peter said he understood.

"Maybe we'll see each other around town, and maybe you will change your mind about going out."

I rolled my eyes and let out a loud sigh. "Bye."

Peter was not my type. I wasn't interested and didn't see myself being interested in him in the future.

I spent the next two weekends hanging around the coffee shop with my dad and some friends. He always managed to pop up wherever I was. I had never seen

THE LESSER OF TWO EVILS

Peter until a few weeks earlier, and suddenly he was everywhere. He was semi-stalking me, and it was annoying. Vickie took note and warned me.

"You need to avoid that one. He's no good."

"I'm trying. He shows up everywhere I go."

Peter started appearing at various social functions, knowing I would be there. He showed up at a poetry reading at the coffee shop and read a love poem, casually glancing my way from time to time. I walked out, ignoring him. No matter how much I tried to avoid Peter, I couldn't shake him. He called my house every day and followed me around town. It annoyed me to no end, but after a while, he started to grow on me. It was nice having someone who listened when I talked after I spent much of my life being quiet.

A popular band made a surprise appearance at a local venue, and everyone decided to go watch them perform. Peter showed up, and, of course, ended up in the middle of my circle of friends. He complained he pulled a muscle in his shoulder earlier that day. I was a caregiver. I had always been the person who took care of everyone.

"Come here."

I thought nothing of it. I was only being nice when I massaged his shoulder. My entire life was centered around taking care of other people, so it was simply a nice gesture. That's how I saw it.

"I'm going to marry those fingers someday."

He obviously read more into my actions. I certainly wasn't flirting, but he took it that way. My cousin noticed and shook her head in disapproval. I pointed toward the door, and she nodded.

"I have to go. My ride is leaving."

"I'll take you home."

"Nah. We've both been busy, and I promised her I would hang out this weekend. Gotta go."

He watched me walk away, and I knew it. I could feel him watching me. Once again, Vickie warned me. I should have listened to her. I wish I had listened to her, but I didn't. It wasn't that I wanted a relationship with him. I just stopped fighting it. My grandmother told me many times to be careful who I spent time with because I couldn't help who I fell in love with. I should have listened to her, too.

Over the next few weeks, Peter called my house several times a day. If my grandmother told him I wasn't home, he found me. When I agreed to go out with him, it was a surrender. He had worn me down, not won me over. I couldn't get away from him, so I thought I might as well go out with him and see what happened. There was no way for me to know what a terrible mistake I was making back then.

He wasn't what I expected. Peter wanted to know everything about me, and no one had ever wanted to really get to know me. I was surprised. He was nice and considerate. We were soon going out every weekend, and about a month after we started dating, he told me he was falling in love with me. A few weeks later, he said he loved me. Soon after he professed his love for me, we had sex for the first time. I didn't feel like I had any reason to be worried he would dump me after the way he pursued me. Why would someone who stalked me for months suddenly change their mind?

Everything seemed fine, and then I was blindsided. Peter called and asked me to meet him in front of the coffee shop. I saw him sitting in his car when I pulled into the parking lot. I opened the passenger door and sat down. When I looked at him, I noticed two things. He was drunk, and his entire neck was covered in hickeys. I shook my head. He started speaking, but I cut him off before he could say anything.

"Don't bother."

He felt like he had to explain, but I did not need or want an explanation. I just shook my head. Peter managed to get in a few words before I got out of the car. He told me he felt so bad about it he had to get drunk before he could tell me. I should have seen it right then. I should have noticed it right then. He wanted me to feel bad about how guilty he felt for doing something that hurt me. That's where it started. He wanted me to feel bad for him when he screwed up, and I didn't see the signs. I didn't feel bad for him, but it was the beginning of his attempts to control how I felt about things.

Perhaps if I had not been so hurt by his actions I would have noticed, but I was crushed. It wasn't just that I genuinely cared about him, but I had once again fallen for some guy's bullshit. I wondered what was wrong with me that I kept letting my morals fall to the side when a guy paid me more than a little attention.

I kept shaking my head as I slammed the car door and walked away. My dad asked if I was okay.

"I'm fine. Wanna hang out this weekend?"

"Sure."

We drove off, and I put him out of my head. Dad and I stayed in town the next couple of nights. Peter followed us and watched from a distance. Friends told me he wanted to apologize, but I didn't want to hear it. After a week, I was fed up with being followed. I called my ex-boyfriend and asked if he wanted to hang out with me. I had been told he was hurt I moved on and was more than a little jealous, and I knew he would agree. He was more than happy to meet me at the coffee shop.

It was an easy way to kill two birds with one stone. I made sure Peter saw me with my ex, and it irritated him. He called my dad to the side and tried crying on his shoulder. Dad was polite, but we had a good laugh about it later. My ex-boyfriend wanted to take me home, so I told dad I would see him in a little while. When the guy tried pulling into a dark and deserted area, I told him to take me home.

"I thought…I thought you wanted to get back together."

"Did you really think I would take you back? I didn't think you would ditch me after you got what you wanted, so here we both are—wrong. Take me home."

Two birds. One stone. I was feeling pretty good when I crawled into my bed that night. Dad stuck his head in the door.

"You okay?"

"Great. I put both of them in their place."

He smiled. "Atta girl, Laura. Don't take shit off of anybody."

Over the next few days, Peter was worse. He was always around, lurking in the shadows. He cried and begged for forgiveness every chance he got. I should have walked away. I should have laughed as he cried. I should have listened to my cousin. That is what I should have done. I should have left him alone, but I felt sorry for him. He had succeeded. I felt sorry for him.

It was stupid of me to feel bad for him after what

he had done. He deserved to be alone. It wasn't just pity that made me change my mind. Peter was not going to leave me alone. He had become my shadow, and it seemed there was no way I was going to get rid of him.

"Fine. We can talk, but that's it. I'm not interested in taking you back."

I meant it. He was the last person I wanted to date after what he had done, but he wasn't disappearing. No matter where I was or when I showed up, he always found me.

Peter was always nearby, but it didn't seem to matter much to anyone else. Other guys flocked to me. There were many times where I gave my dad a certain look. He knew what it meant.

"Hey, I have to go get something to drink. Hop in."

He knew it was my way of saying I was tired of whoever was trying to talk to me. I told Peter I didn't understand why I couldn't go anywhere without guys following me around like lost puppies. He told me about the bet.

"But I'm not a virgin now."

"Yeah, but you haven't been passed around like the rest of these girls."

It was then that it hit me.

"So, getting me was about a bet for you?" My entire body felt like it was on fire. I gritted my teeth and shook my head as I walked away.

"Dad, hand me a beer."

He raised an eyebrow and glared at me. "You okay?"

I cracked open the beer and took a large gulp. "Will be. I will be."

CHAPTER THREE

Honestly, I don't know why I took him back. It didn't seem like he would ever go away, so maybe that was it. Maybe it was because he listened when I talked. Maybe it was because his determination made me think he really cared and was truly sorry. I don't know. I was just a stupid little girl. The world kept spinning, and life went on. Good or bad, it just kept going.

My dad met a woman, and they got married not long after they met. He moved out of my grandparents' house, and I moved with him. Everything was fine for a little while. I got along well with his new wife. She partied like dad, but I was used to it.

It became a nonstop party at their house, and I knew where it was leading. Dad's habits were picking up. He was often agitated, but he was not my responsibility anymore. It was his wife's place to deal with him.

Peter and I were still dating, and we wanted to go out on the weekend. Dad told me I had no curfew and was free to do what I wanted. I gave myself a curfew. I decided 1 a.m. was reasonable. Dad and I never went home before 2 a.m., but I was going out alone. I thought it would be okay, but I was wrong.

When I arrived home, I realized they had a raging party while I was gone. A stranger was crashed in my bed, and I was stuck with the loveseat in the living room. Dad was sitting in his rocking chair beside the coffee table in a state I knew all too well. I could tell he was on a mix of uppers and downers, with each one kicking in every now and then. One minute he was falling out, and then he was wide awake for a short time.

I started paying close attention when he began falling over toward the table. There was no way we could take him to the emergency room if he fell over and cut his head open on the corner of the table. I got up and pulled him back up in the chair.

"Don't touch me."

I didn't say a word. I went back and laid down, but I kept an eye on him. He started to slump over again, and I picked him back up and set him upright again.

"Don't touch me, mother fucker."

"I was just trying to keep you from getting hurt."

He slowly moved down in his chair while I eyed him. His leather bag was on the floor on the other side of the chair. Dad carried the bag everywhere. He kept his medications and various drugs stashed inside, along with his pistol. When he slipped down quickly,

I jumped up and tried to pick him back up before he got hurt. I stopped when his .25 revolver met my temple.

I heard the click when he pulled back the hammer. I felt the cold barrel pressing into my skin.

"I said don't touch me, mother fucker."

He had no idea who I was. None. Dad thought a stranger was grabbing him, so I knew he would pull the trigger.

I didn't say a word. Years of experience taught me there was no reasoning with him in this state. Doing so at that moment would have likely ended with a bullet in my brain. I slowly backed away and sat down, eyeing him the entire time. When he turned his head, I forced myself between the seat cushions and the back of the loveseat. I didn't want him to see me over the arm, and he likely wouldn't spot me if he managed to get out of his chair. I needed to be invisible until he came down off whatever drugs he was on at the time. If he saw me, he could mistake me for anyone or anything. If he saw me, he would likely kill me.

I took shallow breaths so I wouldn't make any noise. I was wedged between the arms of the loveseat, under the cushions, hoping and praying he wouldn't stand up and shoot me. My head was shoved under the excess padding on one of its arms. Parts of my body started to tingle and go numb, but I was too afraid to move. I ended up falling asleep after sunrise.

The sound of people moving around in the kitchen woke me up around 10 a.m. I started to stretch out, but parts of my body were numb and other parts felt frozen after sleeping in such an odd position on the short loveseat. Both legs were numb, and I fell back down when I tried to stand. He saw me.

"What are you doing in here?"

He did not remember he had company that stayed in my room. He did not remember me coming home. Dad had come down off his high and had no idea what happened overnight. This was normal. This was our normal. The only thing new about the whole situation was the introduction of a gun.

Peter called a few hours later. I told him what happened when dad walked into the other room. His response was a grunt I felt was the verbal equivalent of a shoulder shrug. He told me he had to take care of something and said he would call me back.

Dad came down the hallway and headed to the door.

"Need anything from the store?"

Valium, I thought.

"Laura?"

"I'm good. Think I'm going to start cleaning the kitchen."

"Okay then. Be back in a little while."

The phone rang not long after dad pulled out of the driveway. It was Peter.

"Is your dad home?"

"He went to the store. Why?"

"Pack your things. Your grandpa told me to bring you home."

I later learned Peter went straight to my grandparents' house and spoke to my grandpa after he talked to me.

"Go get her." Grandpa directed him to go pick me up when dad left and bring me home.

I went back to my grandparents' house. Home. My grandparents' house was home to me, and it was where I belonged. Dad was too far gone. I know it sounds insane to say that was when things had gone too far after everything else he had done over the years. I know, but that was the very moment I felt his habits were finally out of control. The overdoses weren't out of control. It was normal. Getting high to the point of being unable to move wasn't out of control. It was normal. Anything that hurt him was normal. He had done it all. Doing something that could hurt someone else was out of control. I loved him, but I could not risk my life to take care of him. Beatings were one thing. Putting a gun to my head crossed a line.

My dad and his new wife separated a few months after they were married. He moved back to my grandparents' house, and I knew this would not end well. Our fights escalated. I was no longer concerned with his well-being. He was a grown man, and it was time for him to take care of himself. I had grown weary of acting as the parent in our relationship. Dad still needed someone to make sure he didn't hurt himself while he was high, but I had no interest. It angered him when I stopped monitoring him during his overnight binges.

My grandmother blamed me for his actions. She accused me of provoking him and said I knew better. Punching, kicking, slapping...and nobody intervened. It was something I could no longer tolerate, but I was stuck.

I was wrestling with a deep depression and started cutting again. I wanted to die, but I didn't have the courage to end it. My aunt knew something was terribly wrong and told me I could stay with her. I had lived with her off and on in the past, and I knew I would be safe there. My uncle would never tolerate Dad showing up trying to hurt me. I decided it was the best thing I could do to protect myself.

When my dad and grandparents left to go to appointments with their doctors, I packed my clothes. Peter picked me up and took me to my aunt's home. For the first time since my dad returned, I felt safe. The feeling didn't last long.

As soon as my grandparents returned home, dad noticed my clothes were gone. They knew where I went. It was the only place I would go. My grandfather called my aunt and said just four words when she answered the phone: "Bring her home now."

"Yes, sir," she replied. I knew. I knew what happened and knew I was going back to my grandparents' home. Nobody argued with my grandpa. When he spoke, everyone listened and obeyed.

Peter drove me home. He tried helping me take my clothes inside, but I told him to leave. I knew it was going to be bad. My grandmother was sitting in her chair beside the door.

"Your dad is taking the locks off the bedroom door, but he'll be back in a minute to deal with you."

There would be no more running to my room and locking the door to escape his beatings, and my grandparents would not intervene. That was quite clear. I inched my way into the middle of the living room floor. As soon as my grandfather closed the door behind me, my dad was right in front of me, inches from my face.

Dad's fists were clenched, and he was angry like I had never seen before when he was sober. This was the rage that only came out when he was high. It was the rage I saw in his eyes when he put his gun to my head. I could not imagine how much worse it would be when he got high later that night, and I knew he would. He did it nightly.

My eyes shifted to the gun rack hanging on the wall beside him. I knew each gun was loaded and was terrified of what could happen.

"You're never leaving this house again. You'll go to school...work...that's it. That's it! And I'll be watching you."

His screaming was so loud my eyes blinked with each word he spoke. I would have no way out. I would have no way to run. My entire body was trembling, and for a brief moment, I thought he might kill me right then and there and nobody would bother to try and stop him.

There was nothing else I could do. I had no choice. I did what was necessary to survive. I ran for the phone and called my mother. He wouldn't hurt me while I was on the phone with her. Dad spent a good bit of time in jail over the years. I would never call the police. I knew better. If I called, he would make sure to beat me enough to make it worth his time before they arrived. She wouldn't hesitate to call the police, and he didn't want that.

"Can I stay with you? Like, right now...or never."

She paused. Mom knew if I was asking to come back to her house something was terribly wrong. "Why?"

"He's going to kill me."

I didn't have to say who. She knew who I meant. I was genuinely afraid Dad would kill me. If not at that moment, later that night when he was high.

"Look, if you're not going to come get me, let me

know and I'll just run."

"No. No, I'll be right there."

I pulled my bags back out onto the porch and stood outside watching and waiting. It was a ten-minute drive, so I knew it would be about 15 minutes before she arrived. My eyes went from the door to the road and back, over and over again. I kept an eye on traffic when I glanced at the road in case I had to run. If he came after me, my only escape would be crossing the road.

Looking back, I don't think I would have hesitated to run out in traffic. I was afraid. I seriously feared for my life. I kept seeing the pistol and the rage in his eyes that night. This was worse, and he was sober. It would be even worse when he got high.

I saw him pacing back and forth in front of the door, and I knew his anger would eventually compel him to bolt out the door and come after me. I dragged my bags to the road and stood there, waiting but ready to run if needed.

My mom knew how serious it was when she saw me standing by the road. She knew it was bad before she arrived, but she knew it was really serious. I would never ask to return to her house under any other circumstances. I was used to being the adult and wasn't going to be treated like a child after spending years taking care of everyone else.

He had gone too far, and I had to do something. This could not continue—being at the mercy of a madman or running from him. It was time to devise a plan to take control of my life.

Adjusting to life at mom's house was difficult. I had nowhere else to go, but I did have other things. I had a job and had saved a little money, and I would need it to do what I needed to do. The only way I could take control of my life was to implement my plan. That's how I saw it. I had no other options. I did not see how it could be any worse, because I believed anything was better than bouncing from house to house in hopes of finding happiness. I was wrong and had no idea how wrong I was. At 16 years old, after everything I had been through, I thought I knew everything.

My plan was simple. First, I would buy my own car. I had to have a car to keep a job. My grandfather would not let me buy a car, but my mom would. She wouldn't let me pick the car, but she did let me buy one, even if it was one of her choosing. It was the biggest gas guzzler, but it was mine. That was the first step.

The second part of my plan was to get married and get my own place. That part was more complicated. Unless I was 18, there was only one way I was going to be out on my own—I would have to get married. Nobody was going to let me get married. Nobody. Of course, they would rush to marry me off if I got pregnant.

My plan was not brilliant, but it was created out of desperation and despair. My options were unacceptable. I could go back to my grandparents and hope dad didn't kill me in a fit of rage, or I could stay at my mother's house. For a number of reasons, neither option was acceptable. The only way to escape it all was to create a new option, and I did. I had a better chance making it on my own. I had taken care of myself and everyone around me all my life. At least in this scenario, I would be in control.

Make no mistake about it. Peter was not trapped or an unwilling participant. My plan was his plan. It was our plan, and we devised it together.

Our plan wasn't working quick enough, and the tension between us was mounting. Peter and I had a huge fight one night while I was at work. It ended with him following me when I left because I refused to speak to him after I said what I had to say. I finally pulled over in a convenience store parking lot not far from my mother's house. After a short screaming match, mom pulled in behind us. I was late getting home, and she decided to make sure nothing had happened to me. I screamed at him it was over and told her I was going home.

That was that, and just like that, I was back at square one. My plan was up in smoke, and I had no idea what I was going to do. It was two long years before I turned 18, and I had no idea what would happen to me. I was devastated, to say the least.

It was spring break, and I could not stand the thought of sitting at home and dwelling on it all. I needed someone to talk to, and one of my male friends was willing to let me cry on his shoulder. We had been friends for years, and I knew he would understand.

We spent a great deal of time hanging out and talking over the next week. He tried his best to comfort me, telling me everything was going to work out in the end. My emotions were getting the better of me, and a friendly hug turned into a kiss. A kiss turned into so much more.

After crying on his shoulder for an entire week,

something was bound to happen. Raw emotion made us cross a line. It was only once, and I won't say it was a mistake. It just happened. We had been friends for years, and neither of us wanted to lose our friendship. We decided to put some space between us for a while so everything could go back to the way it was before it happened.

A week later, Peter and I reconciled and ended our two-week split. Everything went back to normal after a lengthy conversation and a heaping helping of apologies on his part. We decided we were both in it for the long haul and would stick to our plan.

It had been months since we started trying to conceive, and nothing had happened. I was beginning to think I was unable to get pregnant. In the middle of my worrying, my mother decided to send me to get on birth control pills. I think it was her response to our very recent reconciliation. She did not approve.

Declining was not an option, but a pregnancy after that would be much harder to explain. She would certainly know it was intentional. I knew I wouldn't take the pills, but it was going to make things more complicated. It was one more thing I would have to hide.

She set up the appointment, and I drove myself to the doctor's office after school. One of the first questions they asked was when I had my last period. I was a few days late, and they insisted on doing a pregnancy test before they proceeded. I fully expected it to be negative. The lady walked into the room and informed me the test was positive. She sent me back to the waiting room to wait to see the doctor.

I was stunned. It finally happened. Now I had to wait for them to decide to marry me off and deal with the consequences.

Peter was at work, and I told him I would see him later that night after my appointment. I wouldn't be able to tell him until I saw him, but I knew I would have to tell my mom as soon as I got home. She would be waiting with a million questions and want to see which pills they prescribed. I had no pills or prescriptions to show, so I would have to tell her. I smoked the last cigarette in my pack before I pulled into the driveway.

Cigarettes were a habit that started at 14. "Have a beer," dad said. "Can't have a beer without a cigarette. Have a cigarette."

My mom met me in the driveway. As soon as I parked the car, she opened the passenger side door and sat down. She asked about the pills. I told her they didn't give me any. When she asked why, I handed her the piece of paper the nurse gave me and told her they said I was pregnant. She stared at the paper a moment before she handed it back. Without saying a word, she got out of the car and avoided me until my stepfather got home.

When my stepdad called me out on the porch, I had no idea what was going to happen. He told me to give him my cigarettes because I was going to have to quit smoking. It was his first response—concern for the baby's well-being. I told him I smoked the last one I had before I got home. There was a brief moment of silence, but it seemed to last forever. The tension was building, and I didn't know what to expect.

My mother had her tubal ligation reversed a few years earlier, but they were unable to conceive. One tube was blocked, and the other was too short to go back together. They told me I could give them the baby and never tell the child I was its mother. Pass. They told me I could get married. Bingo. I'll take option B.

Mission accomplished. I had finally achieved my goal. I was excited to tell Peter, but I was not allowed to speak to him that night. Mom called him and told him to come pick me up for school in the morning because they needed to talk.

My mother and stepfather got in the car and drove to Peter's parents' house. I had no idea what was going to happen, but I knew enough to know it was going to be interesting.

CHAPTER FOUR

Mary Cook Bennett Adams was a small woman with a penchant of theatrical performance. Her manufactured dramatic scenes were Oscar-worthy, and she had most everyone fooled with her charming words. The local gossips loved her, and she fed the rumor mill almost every night. She had a way of telling the most absurd story in a manner that made it believable. It was sickening.

She was a librarian who let loose at the end of the day. When she removed the clip holding her hair atop her head, her strawberry blonde hair fell down her back. She would ditch her turtleneck sweaters and ankle-length skirts for button-up blouses barely buttoned and skirts leaving little to the imagination.

Mary was a drinker, often enjoying a splash of

liquor in her morning coffee. Her alcoholism was well-hidden from public scrutiny. She was certainly not a saint, but she managed to create a public persona that fooled many into trusting her and believing any insane story she told.

Peter's mother was always nice to me, and I overlooked her flaws. My rationalization of her lies was whoever she was targeting at the moment must have deserved it. Everyone spoke well of her, and I had no reason to dislike or distrust her. Oh, how that would change.

When my mother informed her I was pregnant, she let out a long sigh.

"Well, I'll pay for the abortion."

Mom was floored. Abortion was never an option for any of us, and she made it perfectly clear.

"Oh no. She's having the baby. There won't be any abortion."

Mary was annoyed she couldn't make the problem go away with a little bit of money and a quick procedure. It was how she handled Peter's mistakes in the past. My mother was miffed by the pinched look on her face. It was the look everyone has seen on an annoyed librarian—the furled brow, narrowed eyes, and thin-lipped scowl.

"Well…"

"Well, this is how it's going to be. Your son is going to marry my daughter."

"I don't…"

"She is a minor and he's five years older than her. He can marry her and take care of his responsibilities, or he can face charges."

Mary took a large gulp of her spiked coffee. She knew she had lost the battle, and there was nothing she could do but sulk.

My mother and stepfather were angry when they came home. Neither of them could believe her nerve—suggesting an abortion. From someone who pretended to be holier-than-thou in public, she was certainly not what they expected. I think my mother's hatred of her began that night. I'm almost certain of it.

Peter arrived the next morning to carry me to school. It was a Wednesday. My mother met him in the driveway before he could get out of the car. She directed me to the passenger side and waited for me to sit down and close the door.

"Laura's pregnant."

She paused to gauge his reaction. He stared at the steering wheel without saying a word. My mom knew he wasn't going to put up a fight or suggest an abortion like his mother. She could tell she had control of the situation.

"Here's what's going to happen. Friday, she's not going to school, and you're not going to work. You're getting married. Any questions?"

He bit his top lip and shook his head.

"Good." She looked at her watch. "Time for you to get her to school. See you Friday morning bright and early." Mom turned and walked back into the house while he pulled out of the driveway.

He didn't speak until we were several miles away, as if he feared she could hear him.

"So you're pregnant?"

I couldn't read his reaction and began to worry he had changed his mind about our plan. This was supposed to happen. It was what we had planned together. It was too late to back out now. "Yeah. I am."

A grin slowly spread across his face until he looked like a goofy clown. I smiled back at him, and he grabbed my hand.

"We're doing this. I told you I was going to marry these fingers. I'm getting the rest of you as a bonus."

My new life would start in just a few days. Our new life was about to begin. It was exciting and scary at the same time. I wasn't sure what the future would bring, but I was certain it would be an improvement over my past. Life would only get better from there. That's what I thought. I was wrong. I was so wrong. There was no way for me to know I was making the biggest mistake of my life. All I knew at that moment was I was anxious to get married.

We arrived at the courthouse early Friday morning. My mother would have to speak to the judge and get his approval before he would issue a marriage license for a minor. It was fairly simple, but we would have to wait until he was available. We sat in the hallway of the courthouse, making small talk to pass the time.

Mary's heels made an annoying clicking sound when she came through the door and stomped across the floor. I assumed she was there to watch her son get married. Wrong. She was there to protest. She pulled him to the side so we couldn't hear everything she said.

Peter was getting agitated, and his voice grew louder. When I heard the words he said, I knew what she was trying to do. "What do you want me to do? Go to jail? Is that what you want?"

She glanced in our direction and realized we knew what was going on. Her tone changed and the tears began to flow. This was the first of many performances I witnessed over the years. "I...I just wanted to have a small wedding. Something nice so we could have friends and family there."

Mary grabbed his arm and pulled him toward the door. She still had plenty to say but did not want to risk us hearing it.

Peter called out to us. "I'm going to walk her out to her car. I'll be right back."

My mom smiled and waved at her before she left. It wasn't a friendly gesture. It was a condescending wiggle of her fingers.

Our witness was an elderly lady my mother helped out during the daytime. As soon as Mary and Peter closed the door, Miss. Evie spoke words I was shocked to hear from a woman who passed 90 several years ago. "I knew her father, James Cook. Sorriest man to ever shit between a pair of boots."

My mother and I looked at each other for a split second before we burst into laughter.

Mary left, Peter returned, the judge saw us, and I got hitched—all before noon. I was free, or so I thought.

Peter and I moved into a small apartment owned by my uncle. The rent was reasonable, and the apartment was furnished. We could make it. I went to school each morning and to work each afternoon. Easy peasy. I had this. Over the summer I could pick up more time at work and everything would be fine. I planned to work up until my due date. That was my plan. I would soon realize my plans never went as planned. They tended to blow up in my face.

It went well for a while. Peter quit his job to

pursue a gig in a band. He was going to have to travel with them over the summer if he wanted a shot at becoming the lead singer. Peter enjoyed singing. He wasn't good at it, but I wasn't going to be the one to crush his dreams. I told him to go. I was perfectly capable of taking care of myself, and being alone meant I had fewer people to take care of each day. It sounded heavenly to me. I waved goodbye as he left and did a happy dance to celebrate total freedom.

He was gone for weeks on end, and I was home alone. It was pure bliss. I stopped by my grandmother's house every day on my way to work or my way home. It was nice to go home without fear. My dad was awful, but he had his limits. There was no way he would ever hit me while I was pregnant. He was excited about becoming a grandfather.

"It's gonna be a boy. I know it. I had all girls, and now I'm gonna have a grandson."

Part of taking care of myself now involved taking care of the baby and making sure I received proper prenatal care. My first OB appointment was interesting, to say the least. Peter was on the road, and I was alone. I didn't mind. I was excited. The nurse looked at my chart and asked me to confirm the date of my last period. She held the little cardboard wheel in her hand and spun it around to line up the dates. She wrote everything down on a piece of paper—my last menstrual period, how many weeks I was at the time of my appointment, and the approximate date of conception.

Uh oh. There was a problem.

Peter and I had separated during the month I got pregnant. I slept with my friend smack dab in the middle of the two weeks we were separated, so there was no doubt about what happened when. At my initial appointment, the doctor told me I was four weeks pregnant. Four weeks pregnant meant I got pregnant four weeks ago. That was my understanding. What else would it mean?

I was 16 and had no idea it wasn't what it meant. How was I to know being four weeks pregnant meant I got pregnant two weeks ago? It made no sense to me. Pregnancy is counted from the date of the last period, but conception occurs two weeks later.

There was no way my calculations were wrong. My period started on day one. Peter and I had sex a few hours before my period started. We broke up on day six, right after my period ended, but we didn't do anything before we separated. I slept with my friend on the fifteenth day—right in the middle of that four weeks, and more than two weeks after I had been with Peter. On day 22, Peter and I reconciled. I found out I was pregnant on day 30. I remember it perfectly because I went through it over and over again in my mind trying to convince myself I was wrong.

Finding out how conception was calculated, I knew one thing for sure—I knew the exact date I conceived because I only had sex once in the two-week period around the date of conception. There was no doubt about the paternity. The baby did not belong to Peter. It was a huge mistake, and I don't mind taking the blame for the mistake, even if it wasn't intentional. The only thing I had to feel guilty about was not knowing how to figure out when I conceived. I had not cheated. I had not intentionally misled anyone. Still, guilt ate away at me. How could this have happened?

There was no way I could mention it now. Peter

was excited. He was happy. What could I have said? What should I have said? Oops? It was too late to try and fix it. It was what it was, and I would just have to come to terms with it and let it go.

I called my friend from a pay phone and asked him to meet me at a nearby park to talk. When he arrived, I told him over and over again I was sorry before I could tell him. I finally managed to say the words: "The baby is yours." I saw his expression.

"No. No, I don't want it to be like that. I don't want you to do anything. I just wanted you to know. I couldn't live with myself if I didn't give you that much."

He was still in shock when he drove away. I was taking a lot from him—his firstborn child. I made it clear everything would stay the way it was. His child would carry someone else's name, and he would not be its father.

Our friendship was completely over at that point. There was no way to fix things. I was clueless and never realized he had been in love with me the entire time. I ripped his heart out and had no idea. He was able to return the favor at a later date, and he did far more damage than I did.

After I accepted it and decided to move on, my summer was great. I spent most of my free time with my cousin. She lived in the apartment above mine, so I was never really alone. I went to work, came home, and did whatever I wanted. I grew up dirt poor and was accustomed to living in poverty. Not having money to go out didn't bother me in the least. I had my own place, electricity, food, and a job. I was good. Complete freedom made me happy, but all good things must come to an end.

Peter came home, disappointed and unemployed. He couldn't cut it as a lead singer. He simply didn't have the talent for it. A few weeks went by, and he took a job as a mechanic. I lost my job the following week, and there was no way anyone would hire me knowing I would quit in a few months when the baby was born. Peter wasn't making extraordinary money because he had no experience, but it was enough to get by, thankfully. He told me everything would be okay, and I didn't worry about it.

We moved, school started back, and I began my senior year in high school. I gained a ridiculous amount of weight, and my small frame couldn't handle walking back and forth to classes all day. It was stressing my body, and my blood pressure started spiking. My doctor took me out of school until after the baby was born, and I was placed in a tutoring program for expecting mothers. Fine. I would stay home, do my school work, and pick out baby names.

Peter took a better paying job in a neighboring county, and it seemed like everything was going to be okay. Nothing ever goes okay, does it? Not for long. Not in my life. He was leaving before the sun came up and coming home around 10 p.m. Something didn't feel right. His paychecks didn't reflect the hours he said he was working, but I was used to being alone and enjoyed it. I didn't complain. Years later, I learned he was meeting the ex-girlfriend who aborted his child.

It started. That is where his cheating during our marriage started, or at least it's where I think it started. I have no idea what he did while he was on the road with the band.

CHAPTER FIVE

I don't know which parent was worse then—Mary or my dad. I was more than fed up with both of them.

We lived in a small community with many young families. It was a nice day, and there were children outside everywhere I looked. Watching them playing and thinking about what my child would look like at their age made me happy. The moment was completely ruined when my dad arrived drunk. I don't remember what prompted his actions, but he stood in someone's yard waving his pistol around in the air. I had a brief flashback of that same pistol being held to my head.

My decision was made. I waddled back to my house and called the police. There were children around. The gun could have gone off, and someone could have been seriously hurt or killed. He was arrested, and I know he was mad. I was angry I was forced to report him, but it reminded me why I made the decisions that led me where I was—married and pregnant at 16.

Later that week, Mary wanted to discuss baby names. My due date was getting closer, and I assumed she wanted to know what names we had chosen. I had picked Seth Morgan for a boy. I was certain the baby was a boy. She shook her head.

"It should be James Paul."

Mary's father was named James, and her first husband, Peter's father, was named Paul.

"We've chosen Seth Morgan. Right, Peter?"

She raised an eyebrow at him. Peter clicked his tongue against the roof of his mouth a few times. "James Paul is nice. I like it."

"We have already picked a name—Seth Morgan. That's what the baby is going to be named if it's a boy."

Mary grinned at me. "I'm voting for James Paul. We'll see."

When we arrived home, I confronted Peter. "We're naming the baby Seth Morgan. We decided over a month ago that's what we would name him if it's a boy."

"I know. It's just easier to humor her than argue about something she has no control over in the end."

"So we're still in agreement on names?"

"Of course. She doesn't have a say in what we name our baby."

Mary continued mentioning her pick of names whenever we visited. Peter would wink at me and smile. He was right. She had no control over what went on the birth certificate, and arguing over something she could not control was pointless. I didn't argue with her, but I never agreed with her. Several times throughout the next month I said the baby would be named Seth Morgan, but I refused to fight over something that wasn't her decision. Peter and I decided, and it would become final once the birth certificate was completed.

The name issue was settled, and all there was left to do was wait. The last few weeks of my pregnancy seemed to drag on forever. My doctor told me he did not advise driving, and I needed to be able to attend my doctor's appointments or get to a hospital if I went into labor. My stepbrother stayed at my house to keep an eye on me and drive me where I needed to go while everyone else was at work. My mother planned a family dinner for New Year's Day, and he was supposed to drive me to her house that afternoon. That was the plan, but my plans never went as intended.

My father's birthday was New Year's Eve. I had not spoken to him since his arrest and had no intention of having a conversation with him. My aunt pulled into my driveway around noon, and I was happy to see her. It had been almost a month since I visited her, and I missed her. We chatted about the baby for a few minutes, and she told me about her newest grandson.

"Why don't you hop in the car and let's go for a ride?"

I shrugged and got into the passenger seat. She didn't tell me where she was going, but I didn't care. I had been cooped up so long I was ready to go anywhere. Well, almost anywhere. She pulled into the parking lot of a small bar on the edge of town. I knew right then why she came to visit me, and I was upset about it. She saw the look on my face.

"Look. It's his birthday, and this has gone on long enough. You're going to talk on his birthday, and that's just how it is."

Dad walked over to the car. We had a few minutes of polite small talk, and she took me home. I felt uneasy and my body ached. Nerves. I knew it was nerves. I sat down on the couch and tried relaxing, but it was getting worse. Was I worrying myself sick? Of course, I was. After several hours of worrying myself sick, I knew it was more than that. I was in labor. Well, I wasn't going to make it to New Year's dinner. I might even give birth on my dad's birthday. How delightful.

I gave birth to a healthy baby boy on New Year's Day. He was perfect in every way. Peter rushed over to watch as the nurses weighed him. While I delivered the afterbirth and was being stitched up, he filled out the birth certificate, giving my son the name his mother had chosen—James Paul. My son was legally named James Paul Bennett against my wishes. I did not get to name my firstborn child.

There it was. It was Mary's first big power grab. My mother-in-law took the first big decision as a parent away from me. She had given Peter instructions, and he did as he was told. Naming my child was her first display of control and dominance, but it wasn't the last. It wasn't even the worst.

Had I escaped the control of a madman and fallen

under the control of a madwoman? That's how it seemed. The summer had been so wonderful. I had everything under control when I was on my own.

I might have been married to Peter, but I might as well have been married to Mary. She made it clear she made all important decisions. I was still a long way from 18, and my husband was my legal guardian until the day I turned 18 or divorced. A divorce would have reverted my custody back to my mom, and a minor could not have custody of another minor, leaving the custody of James up for grabs. I had no options.

Not only did Mary steal a monumental decision from me, but she used it to weave a web of lies she used against me for years to come. She lied. She lied in a way that made her look innocent while making it seem she was proud of the victim, felt bad for them, or was trying to help them. Her objective with her first set of lies was burying any objections I had to how my son was named.

"Laura is so wonderful. She named the baby after his grandfather and great-grandfather to honor them. Isn't that sweet of her?"

She effectively discredited any claim I made about my baby's name. Any time I tried correcting someone on how he was named, I was told I shouldn't be modest about doing something so meaningful. Strangers assumed I was being modest and giving Mary the credit for a thoughtful gesture. Why would people believe my objections? She fooled people into believing she was a kind and caring person and convinced them she adored me for doing such a sweet thing like naming my baby after her father.

"Peter, why? Why did you name him that? We

talked about this."

"No, you talked about it. Don't you remember? You agreed to name him James."

"No. No, I didn't. We agreed to name him Seth."

"You and your hormones. We agreed to name him James. I guess you forgot."

"No. No, we did not. I remember just fine."

He shrugged. "What does it matter now? His name is James, and that's that. Besides, it makes mom happy."

It didn't matter what made me happy. It didn't matter what I wanted. It didn't even matter we had made the decision together. What mattered was what Mary wanted, and that was indeed that. Mary ordered, and Peter obeyed.

Her interference didn't stop there. The first few weeks of my son's life were difficult, and Peter did nothing to help. Mary had plenty to say about what she thought I was doing wrong. Breastfeeding wasn't going well, and I was often left in tears after attempting to feed the baby. Trying to take care of a newborn, keep up with school work, and move from one house to another left me exhausted. I helped move a chest since nobody else was doing it and experienced some heavy bleeding as a result. I still had stitches—lots of them. Much of those first few weeks were miserable. I was weak and tired, and there was a constant barrage of condemnation and condescension.

When my son was about two weeks old, Peter accused me of cheating. He didn't accuse me of cheating while we were dating or while I was pregnant. He accused me of cheating since I had given birth. It was impossible for anyone to believe I could cheat right then. I still felt uncomfortable sitting at times, thanks to the two cuts the doctor made during delivery. I caught a glimpse of the monster inside him, but I had no idea how horrible that monster was. Why did things always turn out much worse than I imagined? I suppose I was just lucky like that.

I will not say I never cheated on him during the years we were together. I can say I never cheated on him while we were dating, and I had not yet cheated on him while we were married. It would be a long time before I did. He had already cheated on me several times. My assumption would be guilt led him to this accusation.

Peter and I began fighting more often. I can't count how many fights involved him replying with, "Well, mom said…" Mary exerted her power through Peter. The only time I was happy was when he was at work, and I was home alone with the baby. That small piece of happiness was taken away from me right before the baby turned a month old. He was fired.

When he lost his job, Mary insisted we move in with Peter's grandmother so he could stay home and take care of James when I went back to school. I knew it was a bad idea, but Mary told Peter it was the best thing for us. This was how she rewarded him for naming the baby James Paul. He didn't have to work. She handed him money, and he stayed home.

After being there for two weeks, I told my tutor I was ready to go back to school. No matter what I did, I was corrected. Everyone wanted to show me the right way to do everything involving the baby. I had managed just fine during the weeks we lived on our own, and I was managing just fine then. They hovered over me until I would get frustrated and hand him over to them. I cried most nights, frustrated by an impossible situation. I had to get out of the house before I went insane.

Mary was still working her magic. I heard all about it when I went back to school.

"Peter and Laura moved in with my mother for a little while. Mom is teaching her how to take care of the baby and cook and clean. The poor thing just needs a little help because nobody taught her how to do things. She's had such a hard life, and we just want to do all we can for her."

Yes. She told people I couldn't take care of my baby, cook, or clean, and she did it in such a way that people believed she was helping me. Mary had a knack for crafting lies that made me look bad and made others think she was helping me out because she loved me. She was laying down the foundation of an elaborate web of lies one might argue was more damaging than what was going on behind closed doors.

The baby I birthed was named by someone else, I couldn't do anything to their standards, and Peter sided with Mary on everything. I should have taken James and went back to my mother's house right then. I should have told them where to shove their advice and left with my son. I wish I had, but I was afraid.

CHAPTER SIX

Peter was always angry and screamed at me for the smallest things. Fatigue was setting in again, and it certainly didn't help. I was at school during the day and up with James off and on throughout the night. The fighting while I struggled to finish my school work was too much, and I became depressed and started smoking cigarettes again.

I stopped doing anything other than taking care of the baby. There was no point in doing anything, as nothing I did was right. Peter told me his grandmother thought the baby's bottles should be glass. His mother thought his diapers were too tight. They thought he should be sleeping on his belly even though the doctor said he should never sleep on his stomach. I was constantly told I was wrong, and it wasn't just Peter. His mother and grandmother fed him much of what he complained about each day.

My depression was getting worse. I didn't want to eat. I didn't want to shower. I just wanted to crawl in a hole and die. My childhood was spent trying to escape a bad situation, and I crawled out of it and landed in another one. This one was breaking me.

Our fights turned physical, but it was mostly shoving. No matter what he did to me, Mary and her mother defended him. Peter and I once started fighting in the bathroom, and he shoved me hard enough to slam me into the wall. It hurt my shoulder pretty bad, and I was afraid something was broken. His grandmother heard the thud it made when I hit the wall and walked into the room to ask Peter about the noise. She saw me standing there rubbing my shoulder. She saw me, and she knew. His grandmother walked away, leaving him to do whatever he wanted to me. They all turned a blind eye to what he did to me under her roof and allowed it to happen. Mary blamed me.

"Laura, he's tired. He's taking care of a baby all day, and then you come home and argue with him. Just shush and listen to him. Stop annoying him."

Mary also worked to make sure no one would believe he was pushing me around.

"Peter is the best dad and husband. He takes care of the baby day and night so Laura can study and finish school. He does all he can to help make things easier so she'll graduate. All she has to do is study until graduation day. I'm so proud of how they are working together."

People started looking at me like I was a spoiled brat or a pampered princess. My mother and siblings were the only people who believed me when I said he was hurting me. Others believed Mary's daughter-in-law was so lucky to have a man like Peter taking such good care of her. They didn't know he had started abusing me and didn't believe it when they were told. She worked hard to make sure nobody believed me.

Over the next few months, I was expected to walk a thin line. I tried. I really did try because I was tired of being shoved around and listening to the screaming. The problem with trying to comply was the expectations kept changing, and I never knew what he wanted me to do. It was never enough, no matter how hard I tried. Once after we had sex, he asked if I climaxed. I shook my head, not thinking it was a big deal. I was wrong. He shoved me away from him before he got out of bed.

"Maybe I should send my cousin in here to finish you off since I can't satisfy you. You're just a whore."

Peter's cousin Jack had recently moved in with his grandmother, so we all lived in the same house. He noticed the abuse and started checking on me when he thought something was going on that shouldn't. After Peter left the room, he knocked on the door and opened it just a tad. "You okay?"

"Yeah. He didn't hit me. He just pushed me."

Jack was the only person in his family who didn't ignore what was happening or try to cover for him. He tried to make sure I wasn't seriously hurt, and he often tried distracting Peter when he was angry. It created a buffer at times, and it likely kept me from getting hurt many times. I was grateful. He was the same friend who saved me a few years earlier, and he saved me from some of the abuse. He was a great friend to me. Not only had he saved me from myself, but he tried saving me from his own family.

Going to school each day was great and awful at the same time. It was nice being away from Peter and his abuse, but I missed James all day. I had a photo album filled with his pictures, and I carried it with me all the time. I constantly showed his photos to anyone who would look and told anyone who would listen about the latest thing he had learned to do. James spent a great deal of time in front of my camera. I wanted to document every change because I didn't want to forget any of it. I was missing so much being away all day, and saving the memories I made was important to me. That photo album stays close to me to this very day and will to the end of my days. It was, and is, important to me.

As he grew, I was told about all the new things he was doing when I got home from school each day. I was missing too much, and I no longer wanted to go to school. Tolerating being shoved around and yelled at was a small price to pay to make sure I didn't miss all the baby's milestones and firsts. I started skipping school to stay home with him, and this angered Peter. He was right. I should have been at school, but it wasn't easy for me to be away from the baby. I struggled with it.

We had a huge fight one morning when I told him I wasn't going to school. He insisted I was. Fine. I got in my car and drove to Mary's to pick up Peter's younger brother and take him to school like I always did. I made the mistake of telling him I wasn't going to school, and he begged to skip with me. Fine. Arguing with someone was the last thing I wanted to do. We went to a friend's house and stayed there all day. When it was time for school to let out, I drove him home like I always did. I arrived home to find Mary standing in the middle of the kitchen, hands on her hips and tapping her foot on the cheap vinyl flooring.

"What were you thinking? Skipping school and taking my son along with you? Didn't Peter tell you to go to school today?"

"I didn't realize Peter was my father."

"Oh, don't you talk back to me, young lady. Peter will deal with you. Don't you ever take my son along on any of your little field trips. Peter, take care of this nonsense."

Part of me was so tired of it all that I wished he would get angry enough to kill me and put me out of my misery. I was broken and defeated. Months of being shoved around, grabbed and shaken, threatening to hit me, and listening to him scream so loud his voice cracked when he spoke had taken its toll. I no longer wanted to live. My depression was bad enough that I purposely did something I knew would anger him.

I didn't know how things would end, but even then I knew it wouldn't end well. My mother hated all of them, and my grandmother adored them. Whenever we had a physical fight, I started going to my mother's house. I would call her and she would come pick me up or send my stepbrother to get the baby and me. Peter would convince me it was my fault, and I would go back to him.

"Laura, I'm sorry. I try so hard to do everything I can for you. You have it made, but you provoke me every time you walk in the door. I try to stay calm. I don't want to fight with you. I really don't, but you do things on purpose to make me mad. You know it makes me mad, but you still do it. Walking out of the house without asking me if what you're wearing is okay—you know that makes me mad, but you keep doing it."

He was right. I knew it made him mad and still did it. I didn't mean to leave for school without showing him what I was wearing, but I was always running late and didn't have time. I convinced myself I had to do better. It was something so simple and stupid, and all I had to do was show him what I was wearing. I ended up blaming myself for his actions.

Peter was conditioning me to accept his demands and take his abuse without complaint. His tactics were effective. While he worked hard to keep me submissive, Mary worked hard to hide the truth.

"Laura is really putting Peter through the wringer. It's not her fault. She came from a broken home, and she doesn't understand marriage is give and take. He's so patient with her while she's trying to figure it all out. She's full of anger. I suppose it's to be expected with everything she has been through. We just keep loving her and hoping it works out."

The fighting continued, and not one of them cared what he did to me as long as nobody else believed it. Every time I complied with a demand, he made a new demand and punished me for not knowing about it.

Peter grabbed me by my arms and slammed me against the wall, pinning me in place because I didn't anticipate the latest rule change and act accordingly. He pressed his forehead against mine and screamed in my face. His grip got tighter and tighter, and my arms tingled as he cut off the circulation. The minute he let go, I grabbed my keys and ran to get the baby and leave.

"Oh, you want to leave? Go ahead. James is staying here."

He pushed me toward the door and shoved me outside while I kicked and screamed, begging him to give me the baby. I knew he wasn't going to let me back in or let me have James. I jumped in my car and went to my mother's house. She called her lawyer, and I pressed charges for domestic assault, agreeing to drop the charges if they gave me the baby. Mary brought him to me, and Peter was released from jail.

I stayed with my mother for several days, but eventually, his conditioning kicked in and I blamed myself. Breaking the rules just caused trouble. All I had to do was follow his rules, and I didn't do that because I couldn't do anything right. It was my fault. Everything was my fault, and he was being punished for something I didn't do right. I packed up James, and we went back. Peter made me promise to follow the rules.

"I don't know why I keep letting you get away with things like this and walking all over me. I guess I love you too much. That's why I keep putting up with your bullshit. I love you too much. All you have to do is follow a few rules, Laura. We all have to live by a few rules. Can't you do that? I love you enough to let you try again, but you have to promise me you'll try to follow the rules."

He acted as if he was doing me a favor by taking me back. I thought he was. That's how brainwashed I was. All I had to do was make sure he approved of the clothes I wore, the friends I spoke to at school, how much I ate, how I spoke to him, and a number of other rules. The only thing I had to do was keep up with the rules and follow them.

Sometimes he shoved me or lightly punched me for an infraction, but there were repercussions for breaking the rules that hurt more than being shoved around the house.

"I told you yesterday not to wear those jeans. You're still fat and they're too tight."

"That's why you can't wear those jeans. Look at the junk you eat."

"Why aren't you eating? If you get sick I'll have to take care of you. Eat."

"What's wrong with this picture? I look nice and you look homeless. Go change."

"Why are you dressed up? Who are you trying to impress? Go change."

"Are you stupid? That's not what happened, and that's not what I said."

"Do I have to do everything? Can't you do anything right?"

"Look at you. You look horrible. I don't even want to be seen with you."

"Don't ever say anything to my friends unless I tell you to. You're embarrassing."

"She called you a whore. Are you fucking her husband?"

"My friends told me they hate you. They just tolerate you because of me."

"Maybe if you weren't such an idiot people would like you."

"Stop telling lies. You know that's not what happened."

"Stupid bitch. I never said that. Don't act like I'm

the problem."

"Act right, or you're not going. Keep your mouth shut and try to look pretty."

"Nobody will ever want you. Hell, I don't want you. You're lucky to have me."

"You think you're somebody important? You're nothing. Nobody."

Those were some of the nice things. I left him several times, but I kept going back. His words would echo in my head, telling me I was worthless and nobody would ever want me. I was a kid in high school with a kid of my own. Why would anyone want a divorced teen with a kid? He convinced me I was damaged goods and I was lucky he still wanted me. What was I to do? I kept going back and enduring his abuse because I didn't want to spend the rest of my life alone. I was convinced I would die alone if I left him.

I walked on eggshells and tried my best to do as he asked, but it didn't help. There were times when he made up reasons to be angry. He would grab my arms hard enough to leave bruises and shake me back and forth while screaming at me over things that never happened. I'm not certain where all his anger came from, but I wasn't the root cause of it. It was something much deeper than what was on the surface. Sometimes I was just the punching bag he used when he was angry.

There were still times when he was angered by something I said or did, even if it was as simple as not liking the way my voice sounded on that particular day. My tight jeans angered him, and I was often shoved around the room for wearing the only clothes I had.

Mary kept feeding the rumor mill to cover for him and keep me in line.

"Laura tries. She really does, but she just hasn't figured things out. She's so young. And Peter…oh, Peter is so wonderful to her. He makes it a point to look at her every morning before she leaves to tell her how beautiful she is."

He would look at me every morning to let me know if he approved of what I was wearing before I was allowed to leave for school, but now people believed he looked me over each morning to adore me.

"James is growing so fast. He's learning so many new things. His dad just loves him to pieces. Laura is adjusting. Poor thing. She's just had a tough go of it, but she keeps right on trying."

She wanted people to believe I didn't know how to take care of the baby. She wanted people to think I was incompetent and didn't love him. Mary was setting a foundation for a much bigger scheme.

"Peter has to be the most patient man I have ever known. I don't think it's that Laura enjoys picking fights with him. I think it's her way of dealing with everything she's been through in life. He just keeps on loving her through it, bless his heart."

Mary made sure to tell people whatever fights we had were caused by me. Peter was obviously a saint who tried so hard to deal with his unruly hellcat of a wife.

"I have never heard her tell the baby she loves him. Not once."

It was hard to talk to the baby while someone yelled in my ear that his diaper was too tight or not tight enough, or his bottle was too cold or too warm, or one of a million other things I was told I did wrong. It was much easier to spend time with him and talk to him when she went home.

My life at home was bad, but being in public was a reprieve. He wouldn't push me or grab me, and there were limits to how bad he would speak to me. I enjoyed being out in public until I realized just how widespread her gossip really was. People whispered when we walked by, and some felt inclined to speak about things she said loud enough for me to hear. It was hard for me to understand why people believed any of it, but over the years I realized how convincing she could be when she set her mind to it.

"Well, I just don't think there is anyone in this whole wide world that loves their babies as much as I love mine."

Mary proved it to be true over and over by concealing Peter's abuse and misconduct. She spent years weaving a fantastic web of lies and built a beautiful facade to hide the true evil lurking behind closed doors. It was easy to see where her son learned his manipulative ways. Mary was a master of deceit, and Peter had a lifetime of training from his mother.

CHAPTER SEVEN

I lived my life under a microscope. Everything was scrutinized, and nothing I did satisfied anyone. Since I was no longer deemed useful, there was no reason to give me any affection at all. I birthed a baby for them, and that seemed to be the only thing they believed was valuable.

The loneliness was overwhelming. It's odd when you're surrounded by people but feel completely alone. That's what abuse feels like. I wanted a marriage that felt like a partnership. What I got felt more like a boxing match with a referee favoring my opponent and ignoring anything against the rules. Mary defended Peter's actions, and in many ways, her enabling worsened the situation.

If Mary was happy, Peter was happy. That's what

mattered to him—pleasing his mother. My feelings didn't matter. He stopped shoving me around for a while, but his taunting and insults became much worse. He belittled me in public, calling me stupid and saying I had no clue about anything. People stared when he told me to sit back and shut up if I balked when he made fun of me. The humiliation was relentless, and he knew he had broken my spirit. Like a wild horse, I had been broken.

In private, he would tell me our friends were disgusted by me and called me a liar. He made me believe everyone hated me and no one would believe anything I told them. I thought it was true and kept quiet about his abuse. What was the point in angering him by speaking out if they wouldn't believe me? I withdrew and trusted no one.

Peter wanted me to be completely dependent on him. Cutting me off from friends and family made sense. My world became a lot smaller as my self-esteem plummeted.

"I know you like to think you're pretty, but you're not all that. Look at you. Do you just not care anymore? Disgusting."

I started feeling ugly. Nobody else would want me. He told me that over and over again until I believed it. I tried to do more to make myself look better.

"Who are you dressing up for? Are you fucking around on me? You're nothing but a cheap whore."

I felt cheap. Even though I wasn't cheating or trying to impress anyone but him, I felt twinges of guilt. It was drilled into my head that I was doing something wrong. It's funny how a person can make you feel like you're guilty of something you haven't done, but it happens. I was convinced I was subconsciously trying to cheat. I apologized over and over for things I had not done because he made me question myself at every turn.

Did I cheat? He said I forgot things. He said I didn't remember anything right. Maybe I did cheat and forgot.

Brainwashing works this way. Gaslighting messes up your mind. You doubt your own memory and believe you could be wrong. An abuser can convince you of almost anything, trapping you in a world where you don't even trust yourself. When you have self-doubt, trusting someone else to get help and get out is impossible. There is no way to ask for help when you're so confused you think everything a person says is true, regardless of your own memories.

He convinced me I was ugly, stupid, and a cheap whore. I believed everyone hated me, and I was lucky he cared about me. No matter how mean he was, I thought I was fortunate he cared about me because I was nothing and nobody. Was I worthy of him? I didn't deserve him and was unworthy of love. I was completely brainwashed. Even when I cut myself, I wasn't as depressed as I was at that point in my life. I walked with my head down and looked at him before I spoke to anyone. His approval was required. He was the voice inside my head, and everything I did was an attempt to please him.

I was still in school and would often walk the halls in a daze. The photo album filled with pictures of my beautiful boy helped me make it through the long days. I sat at my desk and turned the pages, adoring his toothless grin. I loved him without fear of rejection, and he loved me unconditionally. James was the only thing in my life that made sense. It wasn't unusual for me to stare at the floor in class, teary-eyed and hoping for absolution. I had contemplated suicide many times since he was born. His sweet face kept me from acting on it.

People noticed the state I was in, and paranoia soon appeared, compounding my self-loathing. I saw the stares and assumed they were talking about me. I was conditioned to think everyone hated me, and the unwanted attention was further proof. Some of my classmates became concerned. Cornered at the lunch table, I broke down and told them about my life.

Friends told me I was far from stupid, but one guy made it a point to tell me I wasn't worthless and was far from ugly. He began going out of his way to compliment me and make me smile. Maybe it was the flattery. Maybe it was feeling like I was a real person and not a worthless possession. I can't say exactly what it was, but I enjoyed the attention of someone—anyone—who didn't berate and belittle me.

I didn't encourage him, but I certainly didn't discourage him. I freely admit that. He wrote me letters telling me how amazing he thought I was. Reading how another person thought I was amazing helped me cope with everything else going on. It was a small ray of sunshine that kept me going during the darkest of days. If you have ever received a letter from someone who hoped for more than friendship, you understand the feeling. I needed that so desperately—not because I was looking for a relationship, but because I needed someone to remind me I was a decent person.

In the last letter I accepted from him, he wrote he loved me. I knew then it was wrong, and allowing him to think there was any chance of some type of relationship with me was unfair. Still, I kept the letter in my purse and read these few words whenever I felt down:

"You are amazing."

Those three words were enough to keep me going. It calmed the voices in my head that persistently told me I was worthless. I never kissed him. I never touched him. I never allowed him to touch me. We never even held hands. There was never a time when I even hinted I had any type of feelings for him. That was never the case. His kind words helped me feel like a person again, if only for a brief moment. It was stupid of me to keep the letter, but I needed that affirmation. I needed it.

I was napping on the couch when I felt a hard smack on my arm.

"What the hell is this shit?"

He held the letter in his hand. Peter had gone through my things while I was sleeping. His mother sat across the room, smirking at me like it somehow justified the way he treated me. The screaming began.

"You're nothing but a worthless whore. Are you fucking him? What is this 'I love you' shit? Is this what you want to do? Worthless piece of shit."

When he confronted me, I felt a wave of extreme guilt. I don't think I would have felt more guilty if I actually had sex with the guy. No matter what I did or did not do, I was conditioned to feel guilt. I was taught to apologize for things I did not do. I was trained to think everything was always my fault. It was indeed inappropriate, but I felt guilt for something I did not do. Peter made me feel guilty for cheating, and I had not cheated.

There was no sense in explaining why I had the letter. Explaining how I hated myself and needed to have someone tell me I wasn't worthless wouldn't help. I had no reason to tell him because he made me feel that way, and he did it on purpose. He wanted me to feel useless, and telling him someone built me back up would have been met with fierce opposition and far worse punishment.

The entire time he screamed at me and berated me, Mary sat there, smiling and watching. She enjoyed every moment of it. I could see how it delighted her when he called me names. Her excitement turned my stomach. She once told me her first husband abused her, but she was visibly excited by my torment. It was hard for me to believe she was a victim of abuse when she enjoyed watching it.

I knew the penalty would be steep. I knew I would pay dearly, and maybe I deserved it. Did I deserve the severity of the punishment? Maybe. He convinced me I did because I was not to be trusted. I was nothing but a dirty whore that had to be watched like a dog in heat. That's what he told me, and that is what I believed. Had I encouraged the guy? Not intentionally. Had I done something inappropriate? Yes. I should have never accepted the first letter from the guy and deserved to be punished.

There was a big problem, and I was convinced it was me. Clothing inspections continued. I always dressed conservatively, so my clothes were never the problem. I didn't own anything revealing, and monitoring my attire wasn't necessary when he knew every piece of clothing I owned. It wasn't about my clothes. It was a way to put me back in my place. This was how he told me I was his and he would decide what was acceptable and what was not. Much like cattle, I was property. I began accepting it.

Graduation came and went. I knew I was trapped with him all the time, but that wasn't the case for long. One of his friends from high school had been around quite a bit since Peter and I were married. Her husband never showed up to pick her up from work, so Peter took her home every night after her shift ended. He would wait for her to change clothes, and they would come back to our house later. When I told him it annoyed me, he laughed in my face.

"Jealous? It doesn't look good on you. Hell, nothing does. Maybe if you would take the time to fix up you wouldn't be so damned insecure."

I started trying to do my hair and makeup every day, but it was met with resistance and more humiliation and belittling.

"Who are you trying to impress? Are you fucking somebody? You're nothing but a whore. You know that? Just a worthless whore. I don't know why anybody would want you."

No matter what I did, it wasn't right. No matter how hard I tried, I couldn't please him. When we were in a crowd of people, he would make fun of how I was dressed. He would talk about how awful I looked, saying having a baby had really screwed up my looks. People would stare when he talked to me like that, but they didn't say anything. I took their silence as agreement, and my self-esteem took another huge hit.

Peter often insulted my intelligence. After someone calls you stupid enough times, you believe it.

When there was a discussion, I was not allowed to say much. He said he didn't want me to embarrass him.

"You're not anywhere near as smart as you think you are. You know you sound like a total dumb ass, don't you? You should just shut up so people don't know how stupid you really are."

People always stared, but nobody spoke up to dispute his words. They had to agree with him. Why would they stay quiet if they didn't? That's what I thought. I tried standing up for myself a few times, but I was quickly put in my place when we went home. He would grab my arm and jerk me around, screaming at me.

"You better not ever talk to me like that again. You hear me? Do it again. You'll regret it."

I was brave enough to try it again. Maybe brave isn't the right word. The words slipped out of my mouth before I could stop them. When we got home, I was corrected again.

"Try that one more time and I'll knock your teeth down your damned throat. You hear me?"

This effectively silenced me. Occasionally, I would roll my eyes at his comments, and he eventually caught me. Once again, he let me know my behavior was unacceptable. I tried to escape, but he caught me. He lightly punched me in the chest, and the force shoved me against the wall in the hallway.

"You think you're funny? Think it's cute? Roll your eyes at me one more time. See what happens."

I learned to sit back and listen to his insults without complaint. I endured the stares and whispered comments. After a while, I didn't want to leave the house. People made me uncomfortable because I believed they hated me. They were nice to him, but many ignored me. Maybe they didn't know what to say. I don't know. I just know I felt worthless.

"I don't want to go. People stare at me."

"Of course they stare at you. Look at you. You look awful, and then when you talk...when you talk you sound so stupid. They all talk about you. None of them like you and who can blame them? They only tolerate you because they're my friends."

"I don't want to go. I really don't want to go."

"Too bad. You're going, so get over it. Just keep your mouth shut, and maybe they won't see how stupid you really are."

I only spoke to a few people when he was close enough to listen in on the conversation. He approved of me talking to those people, and that was what I did. When I spoke, I tried agreeing with them or saying what I thought they wanted me to say. I tried hard to be exactly what he, and they, wanted me to be. I wanted to please him so he wouldn't be angry at me. I wanted to please them so they wouldn't hate me.

It was wrong of me to assume it would make him happy if I could get his friends to like me. The more I tried getting close to his friends, the angrier he got. He found more and more ways to dissuade me from talking to them. In order to maintain control over me, he had to keep me isolated. Having friends was a threat to him. Anyone who might feel sorry for me, try to help me, or see the truth about him was a threat. He couldn't have that.

"You know she doesn't like you, right? She thinks you're fucking her husband. Are you? You're nothing but a whore and everyone knows it."

I had not cheated on him, but he made me feel like I was guilty of having an affair. The accusations were frequent. I believed I was a whore and was dirty. It was what he wanted me to think. He mastered the manipulation game, and I felt guilt for many things I had not done.

Attempting to dispute him or showing signs of a recovering self-esteem led to punishment. I repeatedly apologized for embarrassing him, even though I had done nothing wrong. He kept telling me I was hated and should be thankful he would still have me. I was trapped inside my head in a world he created for me. In that world, I was despised by everyone—completely isolated and disconnected from reality. I was what he made me, and I lived the life he scripted for me.

The only time I felt genuinely loved was when I was alone with my son. If Peter was around, he was jealous of the attention I gave the baby. He would take the baby away because he had to be the most important person in my life, even when it came to James. When his mother was around, she made me feel inadequate. She would scoff and complain I didn't do anything right. She would often snatch him away and do things her way, snarling and telling me I needed to learn to take care of James the way she thought it should be done. I was being distanced from my child and was becoming angry.

Mary began sending my son to my grandmother's house during the day. They convinced my grandma I was a bad mother and needed help taking care of the baby. After mustering up the courage, I protested.

"It is not acceptable for Mary to make decisions

regarding his care, especially when it involves cutting us out of it like we can't be trusted with our own child."

"You're right."

His agreement was shocking, but appreciated. I called my grandmother and told her to pack the baby's things. Peter and I left the house intending to pick up James and put a stop to the nonsense, but my grandmother called Mary and decided she would hand him over to her against our wishes. My sister called my mother and they devised a plan. Mom stopped on the road in front of the house, and my sister ran out the back door and gave the baby to my mother. She delivered him to Peter and me and arranged for us to stay with her sister in a neighboring county.

Looking back, I'm not sure why Peter didn't side against me and take James straight to his mother. Perhaps he liked holding him over her head. Maybe she didn't agree to his terms for surrender. Maybe he realized he would lose me right then if he did. I don't know what his reasons were, but it obviously did not suit his agenda to hand James over to Mary. He willingly went with James and me without suggesting we go back to his mother's home.

Escaping Mary changed many things. The three of us no longer faced Mary's constant scrutiny, and it was nice. Peter and I got along better. My aunt wouldn't tolerate any of his abuse. He knew it and was on his best behavior. I decided staying in that county was the best thing I could do for my family. It was enough distance that I wasn't forced to hear Mary's gossip, and I could take care of my son without someone hovering over my shoulder. My plan was to stay there, and I had to take steps to make it happen.

The first step was finding a job. I was still 17 when I was hired at a bar and grill. I had to have other waitresses take beer and mixed drinks out when customers ordered a drink, but I still made decent tips. Eventually, I earned a set schedule. I worked four hours a day Monday through Friday covering the lunch rush. Working just 20 hours a week, I was making about $1,000 a month with tips. It was good money at the time, and it was really good money for part-time work. I had plenty of time to spend with James and enjoy watching him grow. For the first time in a long time, I felt happy.

It wasn't long before I found a place to rent. It was furnished, so I didn't have to worry about spending money to buy furniture. My car was paid for, and the only bills I had to pay were rent and utilities. I had no trouble taking care of it.

Peter finally found a job working for an insurance company. He was in training and getting hired permanently required him to pass an exam. Studying filled much of his time. He became friends with one of his coworkers when he volunteered to help him prepare for the test. Neither of us had friends in our new hometown, and it was nice meeting new people. His wife and I had a lot in common, and having someone I could talk to without being monitored was a welcome change.

When the owner of the insurance company had a party at his house, the four of us decided to go together. I took James to my aunt's home and looked forward to a day out with my new friend. There was a swimming pool in the backyard, and everyone gathered around the pool. Most people brought gifts, and one guy brought him a jar of moonshine. He didn't drink and asked if anyone wanted it. My friend had never tasted moonshine, so I raised my hand. He snickered and asked if I could handle it. I smiled at him.

My father-in-law was a mountain man who always had moonshine and felt compelled to get me sloppy drunk when I saw him. The boss handed me a quart of moonshine, and he expected me to prove I could drink it. Thanks to my father-in-law, I knew I could do it. My friend took a few small drinks out of the jar. I drank the rest—straight, no chaser. Adding beer as a chaser just gets you more intoxicated. Eliminate the chaser, and you can handle more. I knew after the first two gulps it didn't burn again if you kept drinking. I finished off the rest of the moonshine in about 15 minutes and held up the empty jar so the boss could see it. He grinned and nodded his head at me, impressed I actually drank it all.

The downside of drinking that much was I was completely wasted. I laid back in the hammock beside the pool, drunker than I had ever been. My friend was also drunk, so she crashed beside me. The boss told Peter he would give him $100 to throw me in the pool. He picked me up and acted like he was going to do it, and I begged him not to because there was no way I could swim. I was too drunk to fight him, so all I could do was beg. Perhaps he didn't feel like fishing me out of the pool if I sank. Whatever his reason, I was shocked he put me back in the hammock.

The good thing about moonshine is you can sober up almost instantly if you eat something. The party was catered, and I grabbed a plate full of catfish the moment they served the food. Within fifteen minutes,

I was sober again. The boss was shocked I could handle moonshine like that. He made several comments about it and people kept winking and giving me nods of approval. Peter was happy his co-workers were impressed by his wife. He enjoyed the attention he received because of it.

It's strange to think the first time I felt he was proud of me was because I got ridiculously drunk in front of his coworkers, but it was true. It was a good day and led to a really good week. It was worth it, even if I did have to chug a quart of moonshine to make it happen. He made a lot more friends in the office after that, and he seemed happy. It changed him, even if it was only for a brief time.

Peter still had to take the licensing exam to keep his job, and he was anxious. The day of his test, he stopped by the restaurant to tell me he failed. He was going to be fired, and he liked his job. I felt bad for him. After work, I stopped by a nearby florist and bought a bouquet of yellow roses to cheer him up. When I walked into the house and he saw them, he snapped.

"Which one of your boyfriends sent you those?"

I sat them down on the counter and turned them around so he could see the card.

"I got them for you."

I collapsed in the chair and stared at him. I had gotten brave. He couldn't abuse me while we stayed at my aunt's house, and I started feeling more comfortable standing up for myself. It helped that regular customers praised me for being a great waitress and complimented my positive attitude and bubbly personality. It also helped that his coworkers liked me. Still, a wave of fear washed over me the moment he stood.

I began spitting out an apology, hoping it would be enough to keep him from throwing me around. "I'm sorry. I was just trying to…"

"No. I'm sorry. It's been a bad day."

I was stunned. This was new and different. I thought things were finally turning around. I wish that had been the case. How different things would have turned out if it had turned around at that point, but that's not what happened.

CHAPTER EIGHT

The couple we were friends with had an odd hobby. They liked taking nude photos in public places. She had an entire album of photos he had taken of her in various places around the city, and she showed them to me privately. Nudity aside, they were beautiful. One particular photo stood out to me. I can still see it in my mind. She was kneeling in a field of yellow flowers in bright sunlight. The entire photo had a glorious golden glow. She was topless, but it was absolutely stunning. The photo was worthy of display in an art gallery. It was that striking. His skills as a photographer were impressive, and I mentioned it to Peter when we left. That was a mistake. I should have kept my mouth shut.

Peter found the 35mm camera I received as a

Christmas present and told me he wanted to take some photos of his own. I knew it was not negotiable. When he told me to do something, I had to do it or I would pay the consequence for disobeying and still be forced to do it. There was no way for me to know how bad his photography experiment would be, but I would soon learn.

His idea of taking pictures involved shoving random things inside me and photographing it. Objecting wasn't an option. It was humiliating and dehumanizing. It brought back flashbacks of rape and memories I had successfully repressed for the past year. When he was satisfied, he put away the camera.

Peter began renting porn and asking for sex more often. It wasn't violent or forceful. It was plain sex, and ordinary was a welcome change. I thought our relationship was returning to how it had been before the incident, and I was content.

My aunt encouraged me to take a job offer at another restaurant because she thought I could make more in tips. I knew she was right, but the new job came with different hours. I was required to work from 10 a.m. to 2 p.m. and then from 5 p.m. to 9 p.m. Peter didn't like the change in my schedule. He was unemployed and did nothing but take up space on the couch. Playing video games alone all day started boring him, and he insisted I pay for cable so he had something to do. Peter wouldn't watch the baby while I was at work, and I ended up paying my aunt to babysit James. Here I was, working, running my son back and forth to a babysitter, and paying for cable television so my husband wasn't bored during his kid-free days of voluntary unemployment. I did all this so I could come home at the end of the night and fight with him because he was hungry, bored, or tired of being stuck in the house.

Peter was without a vehicle, and I needed my car to go to work and take the baby back and forth to my aunt's house. It didn't matter. He was still angry with me because he was stuck in the house. We did so well for several months, and I was too comfortable saying what I thought. I made the mistake of telling him he wouldn't be bored if he found a job. He screamed in my face and shoved me across the room. I was thankful it ended there, but the abuse started again after that incident.

My days were long. I was dealing with taking care of a baby, working all the time, paying all the bills myself, and financially supporting a person who abused me emotionally, physically, and sexually. Mary began threatening to take the baby, and my stress levels were at an all-time high. My life was one gigantic mess, and much of that mess would have cleared up if he had stopped—stopped screaming, stopped shoving, stopped grabbing—everything.

It didn't stop, and I worried enough that it physically affected me. I passed out one night and woke up in the middle of the floor. I must have hit my head on something on the way down or when I landed on the floor because I had an egg-sized knot on my forehead. Nausea and headaches followed. The abuse was worse, but I couldn't say anything. It would give Mary a reason to petition the court for custody of James. No matter what I had to endure, I decided I wouldn't say anything. I just kept telling myself it could be worse.

After a few weeks at my new job, I made a friend. Peter needed the car to go apply for a job, so she agreed to take me home after our shift. She knew how stressed I was. Julia asked if James would be home, and she pulled out a joint when I told her no. I had never smoked pot and politely declined.

"No, you need this. It'll get rid of that headache and calm your nerves. Try it...but just take one small hit."

She was right. My headache went away. My nausea went away. My stress melted away for a little while. I started taking a hit a couple of times a week, and my physical symptoms were much improved. I felt better. I wasn't smoking it all the time and never smoked it when I had James. It seemed like the equivalent of taking a nerve pill to calm me down, without the risk of a chemical addiction. This was a way to calm down the physical effects of stress, and right or wrong, it worked for me.

My younger cousin stayed with me when she was out of school. Lindsey was 14, and I really liked having her around the house. It was peaceful when she was there, and James loved her. Peter knew she would tell her mom if there was any fighting, and he did not want to anger my aunt. We would go to the mall and spend time with James on the days I didn't have to work. She was the closest thing I had to a best friend since we stopped hanging around the other couple and Julia quit working at the restaurant. I kept her around as much as I could. Peter was still unemployed, and she would often stay at the house and play video games with him while I worked the evening shift. Her presence allowed me to come home without a confrontation when I walked in the door.

Peter finally got a job and was scheduled to start the following Monday. Mary called on Friday and told us Peter's stepfather lost his job. The tire factory closed its doors without warning, and he was depressed. Kenneth Adams was a proud man who worked hard and was having a hard time accepting his sudden unemployment. We never had any problems, and I loved him. He asked if he could keep James for a few days to take his mind off the current situation. Kenneth adored James, and I knew it would lift his spirits. Mary had been on her best behavior for a few weeks, and I thought it would be okay. I agreed to let her pick up James on Sunday, giving me the rest of the weekend to spend time with him before he left. That would give me time to figure out how to get back and forth to work and the babysitter while getting Peter to work on time between my shifts.

Lindsey wouldn't be able to stay much since no one would be home, and I knew the abuse would resume. When my mother called and asked if my brother and his pregnant girlfriend could stay with me for a while, I was thankful. Peter was nice to me when my family was around because he knew they wouldn't tolerate his abuse. I asked if they could stay, and he said it was okay. I knew why, but I didn't care. He was going to work night shifts at his new job, and he thought they would keep me from getting into trouble. I didn't have time to get in trouble with my work hours. Still, if it made him feel better to have them with me at night, I was happy with it. It kept me from being alone, and their presence would keep down the fighting. I picked them up Sunday afternoon when

James left.

Tuesday was Peter's second day of work. It was my day off. He went outside to crank the car, and it wouldn't start. One of the neighbors used jumper cables to crank it. I took Peter to work and went straight to the shop. The alternator and some of the wiring had to be replaced. The car needed $239 in repairs, but the car was a necessity. I had just paid rent, bought all of the baby's Christmas presents, and spent $100 on groceries. I was about $20 short in my bank account, but I was a waitress. I would make more than that during the first half of my shift, so I asked if they could hold the check until the next afternoon. They agreed and made the repairs.

The car was fixed, and I headed home. When I opened the door, my brother was sitting on the couch with a worried look on his face.

"Your aunt came by, and she was really mad."

I was confused about why she would be angry with me.

"You might want to sit down."

I knew then something was terribly wrong. "Just tell me."

Peter had shown my 14-year-old cousin porn and tried to have sex with her while I was at work, and he had tried more than once. He was 23 at the time. I was livid for a number of reasons, none of which involved him trying to cheat again. I was angry he tried to molest a child, and the fact that it was a child I loved so much made it that much harder to swallow. Why had I not caught it and stopped it after it happened the first time? How had I not seen what he was doing? I was angry he would try to hurt her like that. The emotional abuse trained me to believe I deserved what happened to me, but she didn't deserve any of it. No child does.

I punched the wall in the hallway, and my fist went through the flimsy paneling. Once I composed myself, I grabbed my car keys off the end table. My brother and his girlfriend got in the car, worried about what I was going to do. After my aunt explained everything, I picked up the phone and called Mary.

"Bring my baby back and come get yours. Now."

She wanted an explanation.

"He tried to fuck my 14-year-old cousin. He's at work. Bring my baby back and come get yours. I'm at my aunt's house, and I'll be waiting."

I knew what time Peter's shift ended and expected them right before or after he got off work. An hour past the time his shift was over, they had not arrived. I called her house over and over again. Several hours later, he answered.

"Where in the hell is my baby?"

I could hear talking in the background.

"He's here."

"Fine. If you don't want to bring him to me, I'll come get him. I'm on my way. Have his stuff ready."

There was a pause.

"That's not going to happen."

"Like hell. I'm on my way."

"Mom has emergency temporary custody. We went to the judge and he signed off on it. You can't get him."

I could feel my insides burning.

"Like I said, like hell. I'm on my way."

I slammed the phone down and told my aunt. She was angry and started yelling. She loved him, too, and she was about as pissed as I was.

"I'm going to get him, no matter what it takes to do it."

Before I backed out of the driveway, my brother and his girlfriend opened the door and got in the car.

"You don't want to go with me. I might be going to jail."

He shook his head. "I'm going."

"Buckle up."

It was a 45-minute drive from my aunt's house to their house. It wouldn't take me that long. My gas-guzzler had a 351 Cleveland, and I opened it up. Right across the county line, I passed a semi-truck going up a hill and I hit 100 mph when I did. I decided to keep it close to that the rest of the way. Peter had installed a CB radio in my car, and my aunt had one in her vehicle. She was following behind me but couldn't keep up. I heard her on the CB for a brief time, but I shot out of range and could no longer hear her begging me to stop. I had snapped.

There's no way I'm stopping.

Pulling over was my only option when I reached the city limits.

My mother and stepfather blocked the road, and I was forced to stop. I was still livid, but they wouldn't let me pass. When my aunt arrived, they talked until I was calm enough to listen. My aunt intended to report the attempted molestation of my cousin. Mom planned to make some calls and find out if they really had temporary custody, and we would go from there.

"If I have to drive my car into their living room, I'm going to get him back."

THE LESSER OF TWO EVILS

Mom ushered my brother and his girlfriend into their car. It was better that way. She was pregnant and did not need the stress. My mom and aunt kept talking to me, trying to keep me calm.

"You're never going to get him back if you go over there and do something that's going to land you in prison."

I leaned against the hood of my car—too angry to cry and too angry to know what to do. Their voices faded away as I lost myself in my head for a moment. When I managed to seriously think about what was happening and the consequences of what I wanted to do, I agreed to go back home and handle it legally in the morning.

As awful as that night was, it wasn't the worst thing I endured. It wouldn't even be the worst thing I endured that week. Far worse was in store for me. My head was completely screwed up, but it was the closest to sanity I would be for a while. I never dreamed it could get any worse than it was right then. Oh, how I was wrong.

CHAPTER NINE

I didn't go home that night. My aunt insisted, and I was in no shape to argue. When I woke up in the morning, she was already awake.

"They've got temporary custody. We're going to have to get a lawyer."

My anger was gone. I was overwhelmed and just sat and cried. There was nothing I could do except hire a lawyer and fight it in court. I called and told my boss I wouldn't be at work that day. It would have been impossible for me to work that day.

About an hour later, I remembered I had to deposit money in the bank to cover the check for my car repairs. Since I didn't go to work, I didn't have it. There was a jar I used as a piggy bank for James, and I was forced to take change out of it. My aunt didn't allow me to leave without taking my cousin. She knew I wouldn't do anything stupid with her in the car.

We went to my house and took $19 and change out of the jar. I counted out dimes and quarters on the counter at the bank to make my deposit. I asked the teller to confirm the balance of my account. It should have been a little over $219.

"Ma'am, your account is overdrawn."

There was no way my account was overdrawn. I kept my checkbook balanced, and I knew how much there was supposed to be. I asked her to look at the account again because I knew I had over $200.

"There was an ATM withdrawal last night, and a check went through this morning causing you to be overdrawn."

Peter's mother had taken him by the bank, and he cleaned me out when he left town. He hadn't worked in a while and had not received his first check from his new job. Every cent of the money in that account was mine, and it was everything I had other than the jar full of change sitting on my kitchen table. Now I had over $200 in bad checks and not a dime to my name. I could barely afford to put gas in my car. I couldn't afford to hire an attorney, and he knew it when he emptied the account. They made sure to put me in a position where I couldn't win.

I stood at the teller window, shaking and sobbing. Everyone in the bank stopped and stared. My cousin placed her hand on my back and pushed me out the door. I collapsed in the seat of my car and bawled my eyes out in the bank parking lot. What was I going to do? How was I going to get my kid back? I wasn't starting from zero to raise money for a lawyer. I was starting from almost $300 in the red with returned check and overdraft fees. It would take over a week's pay to take care of it, even letting all other bills go. After that, it would take another two to three weeks to make enough to hire an attorney. It would be more than a month before I had any chance of getting my son back, meaning I wouldn't see him for at least a month. He was just a little over nine months old at the time.

My aunt, my cousin, and I went to the police station and reported Peter for showing Lindsey porn and trying to have sex with her. They filed a complaint but told her they couldn't arrest him because it was a he said/she said situation and evidence was needed to make an arrest. They ran his record and told her he had previously been arrested in the county for assault. I found out a few years later he was arrested for attacking a guy who tried to hit a woman in a nightclub parking lot. It's funny he had a problem with others doing the same thing he was doing to me. On some level, he knew what he did was wrong.

I had to get more clothes from my house so I could stay with my aunt until I figured out what I was going to do. When I grabbed my keys off the counter, I saw his class ring on the table. I snatched it up and headed to the pawn shop. They gave me $45 for it, and that was all the money I had. It would keep gas in my car to go back and forth to work and that was about it.

The only way I could see James was if I went back to Peter. That was made perfectly clear to me. I didn't know what I was going to do. I didn't even know where to begin. When everyone else went to sleep and it was quiet in the house, I fell apart. I walked out on the porch and smoked cigarette after cigarette while I cried. The sun came up, and I went back in the house. I was too depressed to eat. I was too depressed to sleep. I was too depressed to do anything. Working was out of the question.

During my downward spiral, Mary worked hard feeding the rumor mill to undermine my credibility. She couldn't have anyone believe Peter abused me or tried to molest a 14-year-old. That wouldn't have helped her case at all since he lived in the house with the baby. She would do everything she could to protect Peter because he helped her take James, and she wanted to make sure she could keep him.

They told the judge awful lies, and Peter corroborated the story. They claimed James was neglected and abused by me, and the judge signed off on the emergency temporary custody order because of his statements. In the middle of the night, he gave my son away out of spite. I kicked him out because of what he had done to a child, and he gave my child to his mother. It was retaliation. He knew taking my son would inflict the most pain.

He accomplished his goal. I fell into a deep depression. I lost my job, my house, and my mind. I didn't care about anything but James. Begging and pleading to see my baby was ineffective. If I went back to Peter, I could see him. Mary would be perfectly happy to let me move back in her house when—not if, but when—I wanted to come back home. They turned James into a bargaining chip.

Let me be perfectly clear about how things really were. They told people I was young and couldn't support the baby, and they told people I didn't know how to take care of him. He was nine months old when they took him. I had my own house and paid all the bills myself because Peter couldn't keep a job. I paid my bills, bought Christmas presents months in advance, bought $100 worth of groceries, and still had over $200 in my bank account for Peter to steal. I did that on my own while supporting an unemployed husband. James was nine months old and no longer took a bottle. He handled a cup well enough to ditch it and drink his formula from a cup. He was ahead of the curve with milestones and was healthy. My son was well cared for, and everyone around me on a daily basis knew it.

The lies Mary told to justify her actions were awful, but it was worse that she had laid down a solid foundation to make people believe her. She spent nine months working on it and accomplished her goal. I was suddenly the devil, with the option to be brought back into the fold if I would stay with Peter. If I was as awful as they told people, why did they want me to move back into their house and act as a nanny for James? Why would they trust me to care for him if I didn't know how or I was abusive and neglected him? The answer to all these questions is her claims were nothing more than lies, and she knew it. Why couldn't people see either Mary lied about me or was willing to overlook my alleged abuse and neglect for the sake of free childcare? Mary was a master of deceit and had fooled a community into thinking she was a harmless lady with a heart of gold. That was far from true.

I contemplated suicide but couldn't stand the thought of never seeing James again before my life ended. Each time I thought about it, I told myself I had to see him one more time before I died. That was how I stayed alive—waiting to see James just once more.

It was getting close to Christmas and his first birthday. I had not seen James in over two months, and I couldn't take it any longer. Everything that happened flashed through my mind. My child, or standing by my cousin? It was not fair I had to make that decision. I know she felt betrayed, and it wasn't that I didn't believe her or I didn't care. I knew it was true and cared very much. Desperation and a lack of options led me back to Peter. I wanted nothing to do with him. I just wanted to be with my baby, and that was the only way I could.

Mary told everyone I didn't take care of James, but his well-being was not a priority to her. He became sick right before Christmas and was running a high fever. His fever didn't break and he needed to see a doctor. She insisted he could wait until after the holiday because she had too much to do preparing for Christmas and his birthday party. I offered to take him, but she refused. Even Peter agreed with me, and he called child protective services to report it in hopes of getting him to a doctor.

Their answer to our concerns?

"This back and forth between all of you has to stop. We can't keep running out to check things over personal vendettas."

Now I knew why my house had been investigated multiple times in the past. There were never any issues. If there were, he would have been removed from my care long before any of this happened. I was

THE LESSER OF TWO EVILS

forced to try to keep his fever down on my own and watch while his health was genuinely neglected.

My head was all screwed up, but I was able to be with my son on his first birthday. I was able to see him enjoy all the things I bought for him on Christmas morning. Still, I didn't want to be there with Peter. He disgusted me. I had not forgotten what he tried to do to a child. We had a huge fight right after New Year's Day.

"I can't stand to look at you. We will never really be together again. The only reason I am here is James."

Peter pinned me against the wall.

"You're not leaving, because if you do you will never see him again. Ever." He grabbed my face and slammed my head into the wood paneling. "You hear me? You're not going anywhere. You'll never see him again. I'll make sure of it."

Everything he did to me, my cousin, and what he had done with my son—it all flashed through my head at once like a slideshow. I felt sick. As soon as I was able to get away from him, I left. I left and had to leave my son behind.

I went back to my aunt's house. I couldn't take the risk of running into him alone. I was afraid of what Peter would do, and I couldn't bear seeing Mary out with James knowing she wouldn't let me near him. She turned my child into a leash to keep me in line for her son. If I didn't do what he wanted me to, he would beat me. If I balked and left, she wouldn't let me see my son. No matter what I did, I couldn't win. I spent my days in a daze and my nights in tears. I couldn't get myself together to go back to work. My aunt kept helping me stay alive. That was the main objective at that point—don't die. I think everyone knew I was suicidal.

The phone rang in the middle of the night. When my aunt walked into the room, I knew something was terribly wrong. My son was my first thought.

"Justine was murdered by her boyfriend a little while ago."

Justine was my cousin and one of my closest friends while I was pregnant with my son. I stopped visiting her when she moved in with her boyfriend and had not seen her in a few months. Something about him didn't sit right with me. Chills ran up and down my spine every time I was around him. Now I understood why. My life was crumbling down around me. It seemed like I was losing everything I cared about all at once.

Justine's mother and Mary were good friends when they were younger, and she asked Peter to be a pallbearer at the funeral. My aunt went with me to make sure he didn't bother me. I was lost throughout the entire service. It was so unexpected, and I was having a hard time coping. As we prepared to leave the funeral home, my cousin's brother approached me.

"Peter said he thought you were looking at him during the service and might want to talk to him."

I shook my head. "No. I want nothing to do with him."

He nodded his head firmly. "I wanted to make sure first, but I'll make sure he stays away from you."

After the funeral was over, we left the county and

went home. Time marched on, and I got worse every day. I couldn't keep this up. I couldn't get my head together to go back to work. Without going back to work, I couldn't hire a lawyer. Again, I felt like I had no choice. He made it known that if I wanted to see my son all I had to do was go back to him. A court date was quickly approaching.

"You know there is something you can do to stop this, right?" my mom said.

I said I would never do it, but if it meant getting my son back, I didn't care. I called my son's biological father and told him what was going on. I didn't give him time to speak while I outlined what I wanted. His involvement with James was not required or even wanted. All I needed him to do was step forward and prove paternity. He could sign papers surrendering his rights and be free and clear of any obligation. I wanted nothing from him. I just wanted to get my son back. Proving he didn't belong to Peter would solve the problem.

"I'm sorry. I can't help you. My girlfriend is pregnant, and I'm going to have a kid to take care of soon."

"What about this kid? Your kid? I'm not asking you to be a father or support him in any way. All I need is to prove he does not belong to Peter."

"I'm sorry."

He hung up the phone. I called right back, and he didn't answer. A few minutes later, his sister called and said he was getting married and wanted nothing to do with the situation.

"Stop calling. You're going to ruin his marriage before it even starts."

"What will ruin it? The fact that he didn't tell her

he had a kid? The fact that he kept a huge secret from her or the fact that she'll see how he doesn't give a damn about helping out with his kid? Fuck him. You know what? Fuck you, too."

I slammed the phone down.

"You don't need his consent to handle this."

Mom was right, but I didn't want to do that.

We went to court several times, and the judge ruled in their favor every time. Considering the judge was one of their friends, I wasn't surprised. A few court dates into the battle, I relented. I asked for a paternity test. Mary was visibly shaken. She knew James didn't belong to Peter and knew it would end it all. Surely this would be the end of it. Wrong.

The judge took a moment before he spoke. "If you're going to keep fighting back and forth in court, I'll place James in foster care pending the results of a paternity test and resolution of this matter."

"They can have him. I quit."

I walked away. My heart was absolutely broken, but I walked away. They won. They had put an end to it. I would have done anything to keep him out of foster care, including surrendering my fight to get him back home with me. Without a court order, I couldn't force the biological father to take a paternity test. To get a court order, I would have to keep fighting while James was placed in foster care. I gave up and stayed with Peter for a while so I could see the baby. They all got exactly what they wanted. Mary got James, and Peter got me. I was broken, defeated, and disappointed every morning when I woke up and had not died in my sleep.

CHAPTER TEN

I stayed at Mary's home, acting as a nanny for my own son and entertainment for Peter's whims. I faced these monsters each and every day to be near James. The situation was worse because they knew I was defeated. I took the abuse. They could do whatever they wanted because my love for James kept me there and ensured I would tolerate it all.

Over time, I accepted my fate. I would be his wife until the day I died. My son was the leash that kept me chained to him, and any time they feared I might leave, they yanked the chain. If this was going to be my life, and it appeared it would, I decided I should try making things easier by acting like it was a real marriage. I tried. I absolutely did, until I couldn't keep pretending everything was okay.

When he decided he was going to start going out with a friend on the weekends, I didn't balk. He told me they were going to his friend's house to play video games. Fine. I would take James and go to my grandmother's house. This happened every weekend for over a month. My grandmother kept telling me I should go out with friends and stop hiding in the house, but I refused until my younger cousin talked me into it.

I figured I would spend an hour or two out of the house with her and then I would go back home. I knew it would make my grandmother happy. If she encouraged me, surely it wasn't a problem. She wouldn't tell me to do something that was wrong.

We pulled into the parking lot in front of the coffee shop, and some of my old friends were there. She parked between a couple of them, and we all sat side by side in our cars talking back and forth.

"Hey, is that Peter?"

"Nope. He's at Jim's house playing video games."

"That's Peter, and that girl is all over him."

I stepped out of the car and saw a younger girl leaned into the truck window. She was indeed all over him. I walked out a little further so he could see me. When he noticed me, he pointed in my direction and had his friend pull into a nearby parking spot.

"What are you doing here?" he growled.

"Funny. I could ask you the same thing."

"What do you mean by that?"

"I mean you're supposed to be playing video games, but you're here talking to a girl."

Everyone saw what happened. He tried denying it, but everyone had seen the girl leaned in the window all over him.

Why do I have to put up with his bullshit while he acts like this? Enough.

I saw Ted pull into the parking lot. I knew he had a crush on me for quite some time. Peter knew it, too, and he hated him. He had several chances to tell the truth, but refused. If he was going to act like he wasn't married, so was I. What did I have to lose? My life? I didn't care. No matter how hard I tried, I still lost in the end. I shook my head at Peter and walked over to the guy's car.

"Wanna go for a ride?"

I made sure to say it loud enough for Peter to hear. Ted nodded, and I hopped in his car. We drove off, leaving him sitting in the middle of my friends who had just witnessed the entire thing.

I don't know what I felt most—hurt or anger. I had suppressed my feelings about everything he had ever done to me and tried acting like we had a real marriage. I tried so hard, enduring everything he heaped on my head without putting up a fight. Nobody can say I didn't try, but why should I forgive and excuse his behavior when he did things like that?

"What do you want to do?" Ted asked.

"I don't really care."

"Wanna go to my house and smoke a joint?"

At that point, the only thing I wanted to do was make Peter hurt so he would feel a little of the pain he put me through since we married.

"Let's go."

I'm not proud of what I did, but I am not ashamed of it, either. We got high and had sex. The guy truly did like me, so for a brief period of time, someone treated me like a real person. He treated me like a guy should treat a girl he cares about. His feelings for me were evident in every word he spoke and every touch of his hand. It hurt knowing it was how things were supposed to be. I didn't have that, and it was what I so desperately wanted. He took me back to the coffee shop when I asked but stopped me before I got out of the car.

"You sure about this? You can stay at my house."

I let out a long sigh. Was I sure I wanted to return to the living hell that was my life? No, but leaving Peter would have meant leaving James, and I wasn't ready to do that. "Thanks, and I'm sorry, but…" My voice trailed off and I looked away. "Maybe things will change in the future."

I shut the door and walked over to my cousin's car. I spotted Peter across the parking lot. My friend was in the middle of the truck's seat, leaned over on him. It hadn't taken him long. I sat on the hood of the car and waited for him to see me. When he did, he rushed over and climbed out of the truck.

"Where've you been?"

"Getting high, and getting away from you."

He had an audience of my friends—friends I had known longer than I had known him. They were friends who would have jumped to defend me if he tried hurting me. Peter tried making it look like he wasn't angry. He walked around and talked to all of them. I walked over to the truck to say something to my friend.

She eyed me, biting her lip before she spoke. "Ummm, what happened tonight?"

I told her where Peter was supposed to be and where I found him. "I didn't notice him until they pointed out the girl all over him."

"Oh." I could tell that was not what she had been

told. "I'm sorry. If I had known, I would have never…"

She didn't finish her statement. I shook my head. "I'm not even mad."

I walked over to my cousin's car. Peter ran over and grabbed my arm. "We need to talk."

"We do? I don't think we have anything to say."

He gave me the look, and I followed him to the truck.

"Where did you go with Ted?"

I smirked. I wanted him to hurt. I really did. "His house."

"Really? Did you fuck him?"

For the first time out of all the times I had been accused of cheating on him, it was true. I had. I wanted to shove it in his face. I wanted to tell him I did exactly what he had done and exactly what he had accused me of for years. I wanted to, but I saw him trembling. I was high, but not high enough that I wasn't afraid of what he would do.

"We just got high."

He leaned in really close to my face—close enough I could feel his breath on my nose.

"You don't look high. Get in the truck. Now."

I don't know how I didn't appear high because I had never been that high before. I was used to only taking a hit or two. He continued yelling for while, and I tuned it all out, humming as he spoke. It angered him. His friend was driving, and it was a small truck. As long as we were in the truck, I didn't have to worry too much about him hurting me. There wasn't enough room.

He looked at his friend. "Hey, take us to her grandma's to get her car."

Uh oh. Now I was scared. He put me in the car and instructed me to stay there. He told my grandmother I wasn't feeling well and asked if James could spend the night. I was too scared to move while I waited. I should have cranked up the car and left, but I was afraid. That's what happens when someone spends a few years physically and emotionally beating you down. You're trained like a dog to listen when you're given orders. I was too frightened to consider disobeying.

When he got in the car, he didn't go home. Peter drove out into the country on a deserted back road. He pulled the car over and cut off the engine, and I was afraid he was going to kill me. I really was.

"Take off your clothes."

I just sat there, staring at him and wondering if he really meant it.

"Do it."

I complied. I was trained to do as he said, and his serious tone was a warning. He shoved me against the door and entered me with extreme force. I yelped.

"If you're going to act like a whore, I'm going to treat you like one. Turn over."

It was rough and painful. He smacked me hard from behind and grabbed a handful of my hair, twisting and jerking my head until I feared he might break my neck.

"You like that, don't you, whore?"

I dared not fight. I dared not protest. I just took it. Memories of my childhood flooded my head, but I held back the tears. I refused to cry. If he saw me, he would enjoy it and it would be worse.

When he let go of my hair, he placed both hands on my hips for better leverage. Each forceful thrust slammed me against the car door. I was pinned, and it made every movement more painful. The only thing I could do was wait for it to end.

I was thankful it didn't last longer than it did. My entire body was sore, and I was certain I had a hand print on my behind. I could feel it burning when I got dressed. My neck hurt, and my scalp was tender. He zipped his pants and started the car without saying a word or looking in my direction.

Peter had done many things, but this was the first time he had done this. It was something I could not tolerate. I left a few days later. I had to leave James behind, but staying was not an option after what he had done to me. Since Mary would need someone to watch James, I knew she would send him to my grandmother every morning. I tried staying at her house to be close to him, but Peter would stop by at random times throughout the day. My grandmother encouraged me to reconcile with him, and I had to leave to get away from him.

I tried staying with friends. He would hunt me down, threatening me and whoever I was with when he found me. People stopped letting me stay with them after he threatened to burn down someone's house if I didn't leave with him. I went back because I had no choice. Out of options, it was time for me to create an option. Something had to give.

It took a little while, but I devised a plan to leave and avoid him. I packed my clothes in the trunk of my car and left. My friends would stay with me in the coffee shop parking lot all night. Police officers drove through often, and there were plenty of witnesses to keep him from harming me. I was safe there, and so was everyone around me. Sometimes friends would drive my car around for a few hours and let me sleep. Other times I was awake all day and night, watching for him. It worked until lack of sleep became a problem. I couldn't expect someone to stay with me day and night, and staying in the parking lot all the time wasn't an option unless I wanted to be charged with vagrancy or loitering. I found a gravel drive behind the school.

Surely he won't look for me here. It's the last place he would look.

There were houses nearby, and I could see the school. It was spring and the weather was nice, so it would work for a little while. I assumed it was safe and slept there during the daytime.

A local gas station had a bathroom at the back of the building that was never locked. When the last friend left to go home each night, I would drive to the gas station before it opened. I parked by the bathroom door to keep the car close while I went inside to wash up. After I was done, I would drive over to my parking spot, roll down the windows, and sleep in the front seat with the keys in the ignition. That's what I did for weeks. I lived in my car. It was the only way I could avoid him and stay safe, or so I thought.

The temperature was nice outside. I leaned against the door and let the cool breeze blow across my face. It didn't take long to fall asleep, but it took even less time to wake again. His hands closed around my throat and started squeezing. My eyes snapped open. Peter had found me and intended to strangle me to death.

He climbed in through the passenger side and had me wedged against the driver door with his full weight on me. I was trapped. I fumbled behind my back until I found the door handle and kept pulling until I pulled in the right direction. The weight on the door flung it open, and we tumbled out onto the gravel. I gasped for air as soon as he released my neck. I tried screaming but couldn't make more than a few muffled sounds. I kept trying and started walking toward the nearby houses.

Peter jumped in his truck and sped off. I climbed back in my car, turned the key, rolled the windows up, and locked the doors. I sat there for a few minutes, trying to process what happened. Once I caught my breath, I cranked the car and drove to the coffee shop. Surely someone I knew would be there. Even if they weren't, other people would be around and I would be safe. I pulled into a spot close to the door and sat there.

Ted drove by and saw my car. He stopped beside me, and I rolled my window down. I didn't speak. I just glared at him. He knew something was wrong.

"Are you okay?"

I couldn't answer. I just started sobbing uncontrollably. He kept talking to me, telling me to take deep breaths, until I calmed down enough to speak.

"Now tell me what's wrong."

I explained what happened. I told him I was terrified the next time he found me he would kill me, and I had no idea what to do. He sat there, shaking his head.

"Lock your car and hop in."

I didn't want to be alone. I would have went with anyone at that moment so I wouldn't have to be alone. For the next three days, he hid me in hotel rooms in three counties so Peter couldn't find me. On the fourth day, he told me I could move in with him and he would make sure I was safe. I agreed. He was really nice to me. He genuinely cared, and I was not used to someone expressing feelings for me without conditions attached. This was another small ray of sunshine to help me get through the tough times. Someone could love me, and that meant so much.

I was there almost two weeks before Peter pulled up in the driveway. I had my car hidden behind the house, and he made sure to block it in to keep me from leaving.

We saw him when he came up, and I heard his footsteps on the porch before he banged on the door. Ted opened the door.

"She doesn't want to talk to you."

Peter did not reply to him.

"Laura, come here. Now."

I knew that tone. He was angry enough he would hurt anyone to get to me. Ted was so nice to me, and I didn't want to cause him any trouble. I didn't want to drag him into my fight. I stepped into the doorway, but I didn't dare speak.

"Get your keys, and let's go to the house. Right now."

I obeyed. Our last encounter terrified me, but I obeyed. I couldn't let him hurt someone who had taken care of me and been there for me when I needed someone the most. I got in my car and started toward his mother's house.

He stayed behind me until we neared town. There

was a pond beside the road with no guardrail alongside it. He sped up and pulled beside my car, swerving into my lane close enough to make me jerk the wheel. I felt the tires slip off the edge of the road and yanked the wheel to pull the car back into the lane. My heart was pounding. He tried making me drive into the pond. Still, I didn't dare stop. I was too afraid to disobey.

There was no escape for me. I couldn't run and couldn't get away from him. There was nowhere to hide. I was trapped, waiting for him to snap and kill me. I thought that would be the day when we arrived at the empty house.

He pulled to the side of the driveway and waved out the window for me to put my car on the other side. He parked his truck behind it, blocking in my car. I turned off the engine and sat there. When he got out of his truck, he pointed to the house. I walked up the steps behind him, much like an obedient puppy following its master.

He pointed to the couch. "Sit."

I plopped down on the couch and mentally prepared myself for the worst. He sat down in a chair across the room, but he didn't speak. He was angry enough he was quiet. Was he thinking of how he could kill me and dispose of my body? That's what I feared. About 15 minutes later, he finally spoke.

"Give me your keys."

I walked over to him and dropped them in his outstretched hand.

"You're staying here. End of story. Sit down."

I did as I was told and sat. I was there for a few weeks, walking on eggshells. My life was in danger, and I knew it. His mother didn't care what he did or said. She would simply sit there, watching and listening. Mary told others Peter treated me like a princess, and she didn't know why I treated him so badly. She continued telling people I treated him poorly, but there was a reason why she gossiped so much. She had a way of weaving a tale so people believed I was indeed the devil. It wouldn't matter who I told about the abuse. They wouldn't believe me because she made sure to discredit me. The world believed Peter was a good guy who kept forgiving his awful wife, hoping she would straighten up and learn to take care of her child. People believed Mary was a kind soul who tried to help me every way she could to allow me to grow into a better person. If I told someone he tried to kill me, they would have likely laughed in my face.

Mary had mastered the art of deception. I can see why people were fooled by her. I really can. She didn't outright bash me. That wouldn't have accomplished what she wanted. The key was to make herself look good while making me look bad. She had to make it believable to sell it. She did, with great skill. This wasn't something that happened overnight. It was something she had done to others for years, and she knew exactly how to sell a lie.

"Did you hear about Laura?" She told lies that suited her current agenda. "I just...I just know she has been through a lot and it has affected her so much. I try my best to help her. Laura really puts Peter through the wringer, but he is so patient with her. We all are. She lashes out and accuses us of so much, but I suppose she has to deal with her pain somehow. I don't know why she takes it out on us, but I know her life has been so hard. I let it go and hope she can overcome it all. I know she doesn't really mean the horrible things she says to me. I'm just the scapegoat."

This was how Mary made it appear I was doing awful things while they kept forgiving me and helping me. She made it look like I was mean to her and she tolerated it because she was an understanding person. If I tried to talk about the things they did to me, people would think I was lashing out at her and ignore everything I said.

"She told her grandmother Peter hit her. I don't understand why she would be so hateful to him when he loves her the way he does. I try so hard to help her, and he does, too. He keeps letting it slide because he knows what she's been through. We just hope one day she'll be able to work through it. He keeps hoping and praying."

This was how Mary cut to the chase to discount anything I said about abuse. People thought I was being vindictive and spiteful if I said Peter hit me.

All of this and so much more was done to discredit me and ruin my reputation. This was done to hide the dirty little secrets of her family. Who would believe me after she spent so much time convincing people I did bad things while she tried so hard to help?

Her antics made me curse a preacher. Literally, not figuratively. I was sitting in Peter's truck in her driveway, and our preacher was visiting her. When he walked over to the truck, I assumed he was stopping to say hello. I had gone to his church for a good part of my life—long before I became entangled with their family. He didn't stop to say hi. He stopped to confront me.

"Mary tells me you have a drug problem, and I

want you to know that I am here to help you in any way I can."

I was livid she would make such accusations. Aside from the issues in high school and the times I had smoked pot, I didn't take any kind of drug. While I freely admit I had smoked pot in the past and occasionally still did at that time, it certainly was not a frequent thing and definitely was not what anyone would call a drug problem. I couldn't stop myself. I snapped.

"Are you fucking kidding me?" I shook my head and then looked him square in the eyes. "Maybe you should talk to her son about the things he does. Maybe you should talk to her about her colorful stories. Don't come out here trying to lecture me over the shit she tells you. You can both shove those lies up your ass. You know what? Fuck you. Get the fuck outta my face with that shit."

The words came out before I thought about it, but I don't regret it. He helped spread those rumors. The entire congregation was told I had a drug problem and treated Mary and Peter horribly. I was enduring physical and emotional abuse at their hands, but I was made to look like the bad guy. I didn't bother trying to correct anyone after that. It didn't matter what I said. Her lies had taken hold and people believed her. I helped, I suppose. When people confronted me over something she said, I snapped. Everyone in the church heard I cursed the preacher, so they assumed I must have horns and a tail. A person can only hold their tongue so long, no matter the circumstances. I cursed anyone who dared to confront me about her lies, and they believed every story she told them after that.

It takes time to weave such a wonderful web of lies that poisons an entire community and church against a person, and she had put in the time. She would smirk at me when she knew others were whispering about me. Mary would grin every time I heard the latest rumor about me. She enjoyed it. Discrediting me made me an easier target for his abuse. It chained me to Peter because I had no help. I could have told everyone I met he hit me, even if I had been sporting bruises, and not one of them would have believed me after all her hard work. She knew she had effectively chained me to her son, and they both had control over me—until they didn't.

I was fed up with it all. Death would be better than living like that, and I no longer cared about the consequences. I left, and I refused to come back no matter what he said or did. I dared him to kill me and put me out of my misery. When he saw I wasn't coming back he filed for divorce. Here I was—19 and divorced. I could only see my son at my grandmother's house, and even then I was not allowed to take him anywhere by myself. Peter would stop by whenever he felt like it. Even after the divorce, they punished me through my kid. They tormented me by holding him over my head and used my grandmother to do it. Even she believed Mary's lies. I was at my breaking point. Married or divorced, they were going to make my life hell. I would rather be dead. I just didn't want to give him the satisfaction of doing it himself.

AMY PILKINGTON

CHAPTER ELEVEN

Everyone believed I cheated on Peter the entire time we were together. Mary said it, and they believed it.

Fine. If the entire community is going to talk about me, I'll give them a real reason to talk.

I decided I would do everything they said I did. Over the next few months, I spent my time doing all the things I had been accused of over the years. The only person I hurt was me, and that was okay.

If I'm going to be accused of being a whore, I might as well act like one.

While I was with Peter, I bore the punishment for sins not committed. People looked at me like I was guilty of things I had not done, and I was sexually assaulted for one indiscretion. I chose to commit the crimes for which I was punished and slept with more than a few people.

Admitting what I did was never a problem for me. I'm not proud of some of it, but I'm not ashamed of it, either. Right or wrong, I did it and don't feel bad about any of it. People had whispered when I walked into a room for more than a year, and what I did changed nothing. The rumors didn't bother me anymore, but it angered Peter. He followed me around, showing up at houses I stayed at and appearing in town whenever I was there.

I was unaffected by his threats. The thought of death didn't scare me. I was 19, divorced, had my child taken from me, and the entire county thought I was the devil. What exactly did I have to live for? I didn't even care if he was the one who killed me at that point.

His rage subsided once he realized I was far from concerned, and he adapted a different, more effective approach. Peter acted like he wanted to be my friend. I knew the game and played along because I wanted him to know what I was doing. I wanted him to hurt. He would never hurt the way he hurt me, but I wanted him to feel a little of my pain. Maybe, just maybe, if I pushed him hard enough, he would snap and put me out of my misery. He didn't. Mary taught him well. He became a master of manipulation and knew exactly how to handle me. I didn't realize it.

I stayed out all night every night, and most nights I was drunk. When friends had weed, I smoked with them. It clouded my mind and I didn't think. I couldn't stay sober because my mind would clear up and focus on the one thing that hurt me the most— the loss of my son. It was too much to bear, and I didn't want to think ever again. If I had been brave enough, I would have committed suicide. I was too weak. No matter how much I thought about it, I couldn't do it.

My friends tried to help keep me busy, and a few tried watching over me. Peter's cousin, Jack, tried saving me from myself. He did all he could, but I was too far gone to heed his advice. At that point, I was a terrible friend to him. He had done so much to help me over the years, but I wasn't going to let him help me get straightened out. I wanted to self-destruct. I believed I deserved it and deserved everything I ever dealt with in my life. Even I started to believe the things Mary said about me, and I hated myself.

I lost plenty of friends and felt alone. The thing about pushing people away, even if it is because of your pain, is they eventually stop trying to come back and help you. Along came Peter, trying to be my friend. He waited for the opportunity and happily took advantage of my weakness. He talked to me like he was the only person who cared about me.

I was scarred by his emotional abuse, and leaving didn't repair the damage. It was naive of me to think my wounds would heal the moment I got away from him. It's not something that goes away in an instant, and the conditioning kicked in again. He made me believe people said horrible things about me and everyone was against me. I questioned people I thought were my friends. Looking back, I see exactly what he did and how he did it, but I was clueless then.

The collar was being placed around my neck again, and I didn't see it coming. Mary and my grandmother worked together to keep Peter informed of everything I did. When I stayed at my grandmother's house, he knew it. She told Mary, who made sure to tell him. It started with phone calls and ended with him showing up at random times.

Peter worked hard to deter me from pursuing a serious relationship. When I got close to someone, he persuaded me to leave them alone by telling me they were out to get me. He convinced me anyone I dated had a hidden agenda or talked about me behind my back, and it wasn't hard to do. After everything I had been through, I was paranoid and skittish. He succeeded with little effort. I didn't recognize the mind games he played, and I fell for it. He knew I would.

The relationship with Peter seemed different because that's what I wanted to see. I found myself hoping we could reconcile. He reminded me of the person he was when we first dated—the nice guy who doted on me and wanted to take care of me. The apologies appeared genuine, and he admitted it was never my fault. He confessed he recognized his anger issues and would work to fix it, even volunteering to see a therapist. His act was convincing because I was brainwashed to forgive him and trained to offer my loyalty. We started dating again, and it wasn't long before I moved back in with him. I believed he changed. I wanted him to be different and wanted things to work out between us, so I chose to ignore the truth.

I had not forgotten everything that happened, but it seemed so different in the beginning. Once I moved in, it reverted back to the way it was before our divorce. The abuse didn't start small and work its way up to what it once was. It started out full force. I hoped it would turn around, but it didn't.

It was too late to leave when I realized he had not changed, and I had yet to figure out a way to escape again. He watched more closely and maintained control over every aspect of my life. We both got jobs at a dry cleaner in a nearby county. We worked the same hours and rode back and forth together. It was another way to keep me under his thumb at all times. If I was left alone, they left my son with me so I wouldn't leave. I knew better than to try and take him with me, and I would never leave him alone to run, no matter how bad things were.

When I couldn't find a way out, I gave up and talked to my mother. Mom knew I wouldn't stay with her, so she got in touch with an old friend of mine and arranged for me to hide at her house until I could figure something out on my own.

Katherine lived in a neighboring town out in the country. Peter had never been to her house, and it would be hard for him to find me. A few days later, it was all set and I was ready to run. I called mom and told her to pick me up and ran out of the house when she arrived. I left my car behind, taking only clothing with me.

I was out again, but I certainly wasn't free. The quiet at night left me with nothing but my thoughts while everyone slept. His words echoed in my head. Being hit isn't the worst thing a person can do to you. Even being forced into sexual acts isn't the worst thing a person can do. Your body will eventually heal from those things. Your mind doesn't. I was convinced I had no purpose in life. I was just a useless waste of air, something with absolutely no reason for its existence. Nobody would love me, and I would never accomplish anything. Each day, I told myself to hold on and wait. I told myself things would get better if I just waited. Maybe I had a purpose.

Maybe I would find it, and if I did it would change everything. My main goal was to keep living. That's all my life was—merely existing.

Two days passed, and he had not found me. On the third day, Katherine's husband came home from work and sent her to the post office to mail some bills. He asked if I would watch their baby while he took a shower. Of course, I agreed. They were hiding me. I went to the nursery to check on the baby when she left. Her husband followed me into the room and started tugging at my clothes.

"What are you doing?"

"We've got time before she gets back."

I was stunned. I had no idea he had any kind of out of the way thoughts about me. I would have left before if I had known. I pushed his hands away.

"Stop. She's my best friend."

"She'll never know. C'mon. We only have a little time."

He kept grabbing at me. I pushed him away and ran into the living room, preparing to dart out the door if needed. Thankfully, she pulled up and I was safe. I was conflicted. I couldn't tell her what happened. She had a small baby and was pregnant with a second child. Her first baby was born premature, and she already had problems with her pregnancy.

Katherine was chatty when she got back, and I smiled and nodded my head. Here I was again, in a position where I couldn't win. If I told her what happened, if she believed me it would ruin her marriage at a time when she needed someone the most. If she didn't believe me, it would ruin our friendship for life. There was no right answer, and I decided to tell myself he had never tried to cheat on her before and he wouldn't do it again. I convinced myself it must have been my fault. I was programmed to believe everything was my fault, so it wasn't hard to do.

My mother pulled up a few minutes later. I needed to get out of there. I had no interest in fighting off his advances again and no intention of causing her problems by exposing her husband while she was in such a fragile state. I walked outside to tell my mom I wanted to leave, but I could tell something was wrong. The look on her face worried me, and I was afraid something was wrong with my son. I just stared at her, waiting for her to speak.

"I need to tell you something."

When I left, I couldn't go to work. Peter worked with me, and I knew he would drag me back to his mother's house. Mary didn't care what he did to me, so I was not safe there. Peter worked the day after I left and worked the heat press I normally ran each day. The machine was supposed to require pressing two buttons at the same time to activate it, ensuring your hands were not inside the press when it closed. The owner straight wired one button so employees could work faster. Peter leaned into the button while he struggled to properly arrange the material. The metal press slammed down, and the heated plates seared his skin. He suffered second- and third-degree burns on his hands and had two surgeries to repair the damage. Peter was in bad shape.

"Take me to grandma's house." I thought my

mother would be angry because she knew I was likely going back to help.

"You have to do what you feel is right. I'm not going to try to stop you." I was relieved I didn't have to try to justify my actions. I wasn't sure what I was going to do yet, but she knew. She knew me. No matter what the rest of the world said or thought about me, I was not a bad person. I had a really big heart and would do anything to help anyone. She knew this, and she knew before I did that I would take care of him, despite it all. I tried to self-destruct, but even at my worst, I did whatever I could for other people.

My grandmother told me nobody was at the hospital with him, and he was not doing well. He could not use his hands, so I knew he couldn't physically hurt me. That was how I rationalized it in my head. I was used to taking care of people.

What was I to do? I knew he was not a threat at that time and had nobody to take care of him. None of his family stayed with him at the hospital, and it was an hour and a half drive to get there. I asked dad if he would take me and called Mary to let her know I was going to stay with him since nobody was there. She thanked me and told me how much he needed me, acting as if nothing ever happened.

As stupid as it sounds, I had escaped again but willingly went back. It wasn't love that took me back. I went back to take care of someone who couldn't take care of himself and had no one else to take care of him. Peter couldn't choke me. He couldn't hit me. He couldn't do anything to me in the shape he was in, so I wasn't afraid. I felt it was the right thing to do, and it was my duty to help him. Loyalty and obligation were something he had driven into my head to keep me obedient. I felt I needed to be loyal and help him when he couldn't help himself. It was the right thing to do, wasn't it? I couldn't live with myself if I abandoned him during that, no matter what he had done to me. That was who I was. That was who I really was—the girl who went back to take care of a man who beat her, raped her, and ruined her self-esteem.

Peter had no use of his hands, so nurses took care of everything he needed. When I arrived at the hospital, he was grateful to have someone he knew to help him. He was on a heavy dose of painkillers and was docile and appreciative. This was a side of him I had not seen since we were dating, and I felt comfortable staying there. I told dad I would be fine whenever he was ready to head home. Over the next few days, I fed him, bathed him, and helped him every way I could. It was a big job.

The doctors were waiting to see if a third surgery was needed. They had already removed some skin that could not be saved. He had quite a bit of muscle removed from the inside of both hands, with pretty much all the muscle removed from one palm. It was a waiting game to see if he would need more skin removed and skin grafts to repair his burns. He was fortunate he did not require skin grafts.

The doctors discussed letting him go home, but he had to wean from the heavier painkillers before leaving the hospital. The fewer painkillers he took, the more hateful he became. The day before he was sent home, he asked me to help him with the phone so he could call his friend—the friend he had chased since we were married—and tell her he was getting out the next day. I dialed the phone and propped it on his shoulder. His demeanor changed, and he proceeded to kick me out of the room so he could speak to her privately. Fine. I wasn't there to rekindle a romance. I was there to take care of him. I noted the anger in his voice but shrugged it off, knowing he couldn't do anything to me. His hands were useless.

I walked out of the room and took the elevator down to the cafeteria. After about an hour, I went back to his room. Peter was still snippy, but it quickly cleared up when I talked about going home. He asked if I was going to stay and take care of him. When I told him I wasn't sure, he said his mother couldn't take care of him because she had to work. She couldn't stay at the hospital because she had to work, so she surely couldn't stay home with him. He was desperate, and I felt bad for him. He wouldn't be able to feed or dress himself. He couldn't manage to go to the bathroom by himself.

Imagine having no use of either of your hands. That's how it was for him. When he told me he needed my help because he had no one else, I agreed. He couldn't hit me. He couldn't chase me if I had to leave. It was the right thing to do. That's what I told myself. I still believe it was.

I changed his bandages every day, gently scrubbing the loose skin with gauze pads before covering it with a special film that lubricated and protected the open wounds to help it heal. It was then wrapped in bandaging. He was unable to move any of it—not even a single finger. It was that way for a while. They told him he would never tie his shoes again because muscle loss in his palms would prevent him from being able to use his thumbs to grasp things. Peter was told he would have very limited use of his hands. I could understand why he was angry all the time, and I let it slide. According to his doctors and physical therapists, he would not be able to fully take care of himself again.

I pitied him, and, over the course of taking care of him, we rekindled our relationship. The pain he caused me in the past didn't matter. I thought about the pain he was experiencing. Taking care of him and helping with his pain meant more to me at that time than my own needs. I truly loved him then. I did.

Brainwashing and physical control were the primary reasons why I kept going back and hoping things would work, but I did love him and wanted him to be what I needed. I won't say he never loved me, because it's obvious he did. He wouldn't have done all he did to keep me and control me if he didn't have some type of feelings for me, but his type of love was toxic and dangerous. It was the kind of love that turns deadly. As awful as it was for me, I was fortunate it did not end that way.

Once he healed a little more, his doctor ordered physical therapy. His pain increased when they scrubbed off even more skin several days each week, and he was angry. Still, I wasn't being shoved around or smacked, so I was willing to let everything he said slide off my back the moment he apologized. He was in pain. That's what I told myself. I could rationalize anything. It wasn't because I was stupid, but because I had the misfortune of falling for a monster.

The next year was filled with frequent doctor's

visits, whirlpool baths to scrape off dead skin, extensive physical therapy, and plenty of pain. It was a grueling schedule, and it was tough getting him around to all his appointments. I no longer had a running vehicle. His truck was a stick shift, and I had not learned to drive it. Mary's spare vehicle was impossible for me to drive. The driver's seat was stuck all the way back, and I was too short to reach the pedals from that position. We struggled to find transportation, but we somehow figured it out.

During that time, we had nothing to do but talk. I had an around-the-clock job taking care of the equivalent of an infant who could curse you out when agitated. I couldn't be out of earshot, and it would have been terribly awkward if we did not speak. The days were long, and I was physically and mentally exhausted.

Other than doctor's visits, we never left the house. I was feeling closed in and needed some time out to relax. I frequently asked if he wanted to go to the mall after leaving physical therapy, just to have somewhere to go. He always said he was tired and in too much pain after his whirlpool scrubs. I was certain he was, so I didn't push when I asked and he declined.

One of the days we were unsuccessful in our search for a ride, he called a female friend of his as a last resort. I suspected something between them previously, and I didn't want to spend the day with the two of them. It sounds silly that I would let them go alone if I was suspicious. He needed proper medical care, and if he had to ride with someone he likely slept with while we were married to get it, it was necessary. I just didn't want to be around them together.

I had Jane drop me off at my grandmother's home on their way. I waited and waited. They were late getting back. When I questioned him about it, he told me all about his fun-filled day. He asked her to take him to the mall while they were out. They went to hang out because he needed time out of the house. I was extremely agitated and let him know. He was angry, but there wasn't much he could do about it. He couldn't physically attack me, so he started working to convince me I was crazy.

Peter insisted nothing ever happened between them and I was some sort of lunatic with wild and crazy ideas. My cousin was once married to Jane. I spoke to him a few months later, and he told me he divorced her because he couldn't keep her away from Peter. It confirmed my suspicions, but I went back and forth between the truth and the brainwashing that made me believe his denials.

I spent much of my time thinking I was crazy. He did things and convinced me I imagined it. Peter would convince me it was all in my head until it happened again or someone else would talk about it. I started telling my mother about things that happened so I could remember what was really going on when he twisted the truth.

This is what emotional abuse does. You question your own memory and things you've seen with your own eyes. You second guess everything you know, and sometimes you believe you've done things you haven't or didn't do things you have.

It was only after I escaped it all and didn't have Peter and Mary in my ear twisting the truth that I realized this. It wasn't until I was away from it all that I recognized how deep the brainwashing went. If he cheated, he projected it onto me and punished me for what he had done. Anything he did was projected onto me, and even if I had done nothing wrong he could make me feel guilty. I would apologize to him time and time again—not for things I had done, but for things he did and blamed on me. That's what emotional abuse does. It wrecks your self-esteem, steals your sanity, and destroys the truth in favor of a manufactured version of reality that suits the tormentor.

The biggest reason a person stays when they are emotionally abused is because they believe it's their fault. They believe the person abusing them is all they have. As sick as it sounds, I stayed. I went back and stayed over and over again because I was convinced I was wrong and imagined everything that happened to me.

Something eventually triggered the memories I suppressed and caused occasional flashbacks. Every painful memory came back to me over time. I never wanted any of those memories. When they came flooding back, it was more than I could bear. I wish I didn't remember. I wish it was all a dream. I wish I had imagined it all, because being crazy enough to imagine all these things would be far better than having endured what I did.

CHAPTER TWELVE

I considered leaving when his bandages were removed. The skin healed enough he could do small tasks, and he was gaining more usage. He wouldn't have to close his fist to hit me, and the skin had healed enough it wouldn't cause him pain if he slapped me. There were still things Peter couldn't do, and I couldn't bring myself to leave him unable to fully take care of himself during the day. I stayed and hoped for the best. Over the next few months, he regained most of the use of his hands. He eventually regained full function, exceeding all expectations.

Boredom set in after his weekly appointments ended, and Peter became increasingly agitated. I was with him all the time. The frequent trips to physical therapy were a thing of the past, so I didn't get a break. He was no longer going to appointments and running around with his friend. Peter had so much free time he had to find something to do, and I was always there. He didn't hit me, but he tormented me in other ways. I was never out of his sight, yet he accused me of cheating. He nagged at me until I felt guilty. I had done nothing wrong, but I constantly apologized. I was afraid to speak because my words were twisted and used against me.

I left one day out of the blue. I had done what was needed to help him, and he was finally able to take care of himself. No matter how much I wanted things to work, it wasn't going to change. I needed to get out before it escalated to physical abuse again. I knew how it worked, and it was getting close. The real issue was I was used to being around my son, and that was something I couldn't have when I left Peter. I had to choose between my safety and my son. It was never easy, and it never got any easier, but I couldn't endure more abuse.

Once again, I found ways to cope with the separation. I drank, smoked pot, and was out with friends all night most nights. Staying at my grandmother's house was not ideal, but I often ended up there during the day because I had nowhere else to go. Peter was driving again and would show up at random times. He would call every day. If I refused to talk to him, he would drive over and walk right in the front door. With her help, he tracked everything I did.

I no longer had a vehicle, so I couldn't live in my car and hide. Lacking a long-term solution, I hopped around from house to house. I was at the coffee shop every night, and I would go home with whoever would let me stay. He didn't show up at anyone's house, but he found ways to torment me. He used the same method of attack as he had many times—he went after my self-esteem.

When I felt more like a normal person, it made it harder for him to keep me under control. He had to change that. Peter would find out who I was hanging out with and would start telling tales. Mary taught him well.

"Your friend told a friend of mine you were a homeless hag, always begging for a place to stay."

"That guy you're dating? He told my friends that he was with a lot of skanks in the past, but you were the biggest whore he had ever been with. Said you were loose as hell."

"Saw the new guy you're talking to out with this girl I know the other night."

Then he reeled me in by employing a tactic he used many times in the past.

"This guy I know told everyone you're a prostitute. Sure, you sleep around, but you're not charging for it. I told him you had more self-respect than that and he better keep his mouth shut."

It was a barbed statement, designed to make me feel like he was defending me and on my side while attacking me at the same time. He learned this from his mother. It was the same technique she used to discredit me and hide what her son did to me. He perfected it over time and was much better at it than before.

"People were talking about how awful you look. Somebody said they thought you were on drugs. I told them you might have let yourself go, but you aren't on any of that shit. I told them they better not say anything else about you."

Every statement was designed to appear like he defended me while killing any confidence I had. I dated a few more people, trying to break free from his hold on me. He had a story to tell about each one. Peter poisoned me against so many people. I stayed high as much as I could in an attempt to drown out everything, but it was useless. I hated myself and became dependent on the few nice words he slipped into his insults. Peter had me again, and he knew it. He successfully convinced me he was the only one on my side.

A person can physically escape someone who has emotionally abused them, but that person remains in their head and can often reel them back in whenever they desire. Years of emotional abuse made it easy to beat me down and take control of me. I knew what was happening, but I couldn't stop it. He convinced me nobody wanted me for anything more than sex. When people looked at me, my skin felt like it was burning. I wondered what they were thinking and thought they hated me. Every time someone looked my way while they talked, I assumed they were talking about me. No matter how nice someone was, I felt they hated me and talked about me behind my back. I believed Peter was the only person who cared anything about me, so I gave up and went back.

Peter found a job and rented a house. We had a couch, a bed, a couple of lamps, and a radio. He worked third shift and didn't want me to work. It was easier to keep me under control if he kept me isolated. I was so bored I mopped the floors several times a night. There were never any dirty dishes in my sink. Mop and wash dishes—that was all I had to do other than sing along with the radio. Since I spent a great deal of time cleaning, I became agitated when something was out of place.

Over time we bought various pieces for the house: a kitchen table, a bedding set, new towels, more cookware, and other things. When he received a settlement for his accident, he bought a living room suite. Everything in the house was color-coordinated. I was obsessive about how things were. I had small knick-knacks on shelves, and he would move them an inch to see how long it would take me to notice. I always knew as soon as I walked past the shelves. He got a kick out of moving things around to agitate me. It didn't make me mad. It was a big game.

We finally had a television, and he bought a satellite. I cooked, cleaned, and watched television. That was it. Since he worked nights, we never went out, even though we had a little money. I was lonely, and he knew that was problematic for him. He adopted a cat so I wouldn't feel so alone at home. It was nice to have that companionship, and it helped for a while. I would talk to the cat all night sometimes, but I needed someone who could talk back and carry on a conversation.

Peter's cousin moved in with us again, and I was happy to have someone to talk to while he was gone to work. Jack had a big music collection, and we would sort through the discs and play music while talking about life. When he started seeing someone, she would come visit and I had someone new to talk to. It was nice. Peter was being nice, and I wasn't alone anymore. I had my cat, Jack, and Jack's girlfriend.

No matter how good things seemed at that time, there was still a huge hole in my heart. My son was still gone, and it left a void that nothing could fill. Sometimes I would sit and think about how things would be if he was there with me. I was getting depressed again with this running around in my head, and Peter noticed.

He started looking for a new job because he wanted be home at night. When he found a job working first shift that paid decent money, he took it. We still had money in the bank from his settlement, and we were okay financially. Since he was working day shift, we could get out and do things. We occasionally did things together, but he preferred to do things apart. I started hanging out with a new friend, and she was at my house quite often. He would encourage me to go out with Maddie on the weekends so he could go out with his friends.

At first, I didn't have a problem with it. Then I started hearing people talk about him. I knew something wasn't right and confronted him about it. He started throwing money at me to get out of his hair on the weekends. He would toss a $100 bill at me and tell me to call my friend and go do something. When I asked where he was going, he would only say he was going out with one of his cousins. Maddie kept telling me something wasn't right. I saw her more often than I saw Peter.

I confronted him and told him I couldn't deal with the way things were between us. It had gone so well for a while, and I didn't want it to change. He started spending more time with me and begging me to have a baby. I wanted a baby. I did, and he knew it. His role in helping his mother take James from me made me fearful of having another child with him, but he begged for months and promised me he would be a better person. Peter kept telling me it would help with my depression over James. I believed him, and I stopped taking birth control pills. When I found out I was pregnant, he was excited. Maddie was not.

"He's going to start acting the same way he did before since he has you trapped."

I didn't believe it. He was being too nice. It was going well, and we were going to have a baby. Getting married seemed like the sensible thing to do, and I married him a second time. The honeymoon phase ended a few weeks later. He started throwing money at me again.

Peter would come home early in the morning; stumbling and agitated. He was always terribly drunk when he got home. Always. Jack moved out and I didn't want to be home alone, so I would go to the coffee shop with Maddie when he went out. I would call from pay phones to see if he was home and usually gave up around 1 or 2 a.m. when exhaustion hit. When I got home, I sat on the couch and watched television until I drifted off to sleep.

The door would slam shut and wake me when he arrived home, and I would ask why he was so late. The arguing started mild and escalated. It became a weekly routine, and I had grown tired of it.

When I was about five months pregnant, he came home around 4 a.m. one weekend. I was tired and had felt ill for days.

"I'm going to end up home alone when I go into labor, and I'm going to be raising the baby alone because you'll never be home."

I walked into the bedroom, slamming the door behind me. His agitation turned to anger, and he flew into the room and shoved me from behind. I was grateful we had a waterbed because I fell on my pregnant belly.

"Peter, you're going to hurt the baby."

"It's probably not mine anyway."

I struggled to turn over and sit up, but he kept me from getting out of bed. He ordered me to stay still while he took off his clothes. I tried to stand up, but he placed his hands on my shoulders and pushed me down each time I did. When Peter shoved me hard enough to push me across the bed, I stopped fighting. He crawled into the bed and climbed on top of me.

"You're nothing but a whore, and I'm going to treat you like one."

I was afraid. I was pregnant and was afraid for the baby. He forcefully entered me, slamming against me hard enough to bang my head on the wall with each thrust. I struggled to get away and managed to inch the upper part of my body out from under him. He grabbed my hair and one shoulder and turned me over on the bed. I had my weight and his on top of my belly and couldn't crawl out from under him. All I could do was endure his violent thrusts. I was in pain, but I was more worried about what he was doing to the baby than what he was doing to me. The physical pain was overshadowed by fear. I was terrified he was killing the baby.

Peter finally finished and climbed off me. He crawled to his side of the bed and pulled me to him, throwing his arm over me to hold me in place. I laid there quietly until he passed out. He was drunk enough I could gently wiggle out without waking him.

THE LESSER OF TWO EVILS

I tiptoed out of the room and down the hallway to the bathroom, locking the door behind me before I turned on the light. The bright light highlighted the red fingerprints on my shoulders. I was cramping and spotting.

The stinging made me wince when I climbed in the hot bath. I eased into the water and moved down until it covered most of my belly. It was far too early for the baby to survive if I went into early labor, and that was my primary concern. The warmth eased the cramping, and I thought everything would be okay. I pulled the drain plug when the water turned cold and sat there until it drained. I was still spotting when I dried off. I grabbed a pad from the bathroom cabinet and hoped everything would be okay.

Why did I stay? I stayed for the same reason a whipped puppy keeps returning to its master when called—I was trained to stay. I was trained to believe I did something to cause it, and no matter what happened it was my fault. I was trained and had just been reminded of why I was afraid of what would happen if I didn't obey.

Of all the things he had done to me, it was by far the worst. It was the worst because I feared what might happen to my baby. I grabbed a blanket out of the spare bedroom and tossed it on the couch as I waddled past it. It hurt to walk. I carefully closed the bedroom door, but I knew he had been out long enough he wouldn't wake until he sobered up in a few hours. The cramps were mild, but I had a sharp pain between my legs. My shoulders ached from being pinned down, but it was the least painful injury I had to cope with at that moment. I closed my eyes. A thousand things flooded my mind, but I kept coming back to one question: "What about the baby?"

The sound of the television woke me up. I opened my eyes and saw him sitting in the recliner beside the couch. I was afraid of what he was going to say or do.

"Finally, you're awake. Wanna go get something to eat? I'm starving."

Peter acted as if nothing ever happened. I nodded my head, too afraid to speak and risk angering him again. He brought me flowers after work the next day. After that, I received flowers every time he did something bad. It was his way of apologizing without actually apologizing or admitting he did something wrong.

Mary would brag about how often he gave me flowers.

"Peter is so sweet to Laura. He just adores her. She gets flowers all the time."

I hated receiving flowers for many years, and I would have gladly given Mary every single bouquet he ever sent me.

When I saw my obstetrician a few days later, my blood pressure was elevated and I was told to take it easy for a few days. I was grateful everything else was fine and thankful I was placed on bed rest. It gave me time to relax and let my body heal after the trauma. I recovered, and the baby was fine. No matter how bad it was, it could have been much worse. That is what I kept telling myself—it could have been much, much worse.

CHAPTER THIRTEEN

My mother bought a new house, and her old house sat empty. She offered to rent it to me for less than what we paid in rent at the time, and we jumped at the opportunity. I felt it gave me a slight advantage. If I grew mentally strong enough to break free from him, it would be much easier to put him out of my mother's house.

Part of the house was heavily damaged a week after we moved in when a storm knocked down an old white oak tree. My mother was at the house every day over the next month while the construction crew made repairs. He was a lot nicer knowing she would be there all the time, and I knew moving was the right decision.

Faith Leann Bennett was born a month later. My

grandmother stayed with me for the first few days while he worked. She pointed out how agitated he was every time the baby cried. He was annoyed whenever she made any kind of noise. Leann was just a newborn, and it worried me that he was already irritated by her.

Peter lost his job. Our car was repossessed, and we were seriously struggling. It all happened before she was three months old. We had a new baby and had to have money to take care of her. Since he was chronically unemployed, I was concerned he wouldn't go back to work. I was pleasantly surprised when he started looking for a job.

We bought another car, but it was a stick shift. Since we only had one car, I had to learn to drive it in a short period of time. It was about a 45-minute drive to where he worked, and I drove him back and forth after I learned. He worked second shift, often with overtime, so I usually picked him up at 1 a.m. I would wake the baby in the middle of the night and go. It became our routine.

Mary brought James back to me a few months after Leann was born. He was going to live with his sister and us. I was thrilled to have him back, and we spent a lot of time playing with his toys and reading books. I tried teaching him letters and numbers, but he wasn't interested. He was afraid. Peter was always angry at him, and at three years old he was stressed to the point of frequent tears.

Over the next few weeks, Peter constantly screamed at him and spanked him much harder than he should. I was afraid he would really hurt him. James often laid on the floor and cried for an hour or more at a time. He was terrified of Peter and was miserable. I wasn't physically strong enough to protect him. I tried stopping him, but I couldn't. He was abusive when he dealt with James, and I wasn't strong enough to keep him safe.

By his fourth birthday, I had all I could take. I couldn't save him, and I knew it. There was nothing I wanted more than to have both children with me, but not like that. Allowing him to remain in a dangerous situation just so I could keep him with me would be a horrible, selfish act. We had his birthday party at his grandmother's home, and he was thrilled to be with his grandfather. I didn't want to do it, but I knew what I needed to do. A few days after his birthday, I took him back to Mary and Kenneth. I told her it was the best thing for him because I couldn't protect him.

"Protect him from what?"

I ignored Mary.

"Kenneth, you'll keep him safe, won't you?"

His serious look told me what I already knew to be true. A quick nod assured me he would be okay.

It was one of the hardest things I had to—willingly walk away from James after everything that happened. I felt I had no choice. What else could I do? It was the only way I could keep him safe from Peter. I wasn't strong enough to protect him at that point in time. I wept for days, wondering if I made the right choice. I wanted him to be with me, but I wanted him to be safe. I couldn't have both.

James still spent the night from time to time, and another piece of me died each time I took him back to Mary's house. I hoped Peter would change and stop hurting him, but he didn't. He was far too rough with him. His safety was more important than my feelings, and his needs outweighed my desires. I did what I needed to do, and I do not regret it. Yet again, I sacrificed a big piece of my heart to keep him safe. How many times would I have to rip my own heart out over him? How many times would he be torn away from me because of the actions of Peter or Mary? The answer would be frequently and repeatedly over the years to come.

It all weighed on me until I couldn't deal with it anymore. He had not yet tried to hurt Leann. I knew it was only a matter of time before he did. I told Peter it was over, but I would allow him to stay until after the Easter holiday. There I was, being way too nice to someone who put me through hell. I told him he would need to be out right after the holiday weekend. Peter didn't leave, but the way things were at that time was fine with me. I didn't push it. He decided to distance himself from Leann and me, and it made life much easier.

Peter worked all night and slept all day. His idea of spending time with the baby was to take her to the store every Friday and buy her a toy. I didn't mind. He was always agitated with Leann when she was fussy, and it was much nicer when he wasn't there. She would crawl over to him, and he would push her away. He didn't want to deal with her—at all. That was fine. I preferred him to stay away from her, and I more than made up for it.

He still let me drive him back and forth to work so I could keep the car. When I dropped him off at work, I would take Leann to the state park and walk the trails around the lake if the weather was nice. She enjoyed being outdoors, so we went every day we could. When it rained, I would often take her shopping. She had a closet full of beautiful clothes.

THE LESSER OF TWO EVILS

Sometimes we would visit my grandmother, but we usually went home and played with her toys. My mother would stop by when we were home. It was nice. It was like it was just the two of us.

Peter and I continued living mostly separate lives. I was offered an opportunity to babysit. Landon was a few months younger than Leann, but I knew I could handle both of them. Besides, I needed money of my own and this was the only way I could make money and be with Leann all the time. I trusted no one with her. After everything that happened with James, I kept her close to me.

I got very little sleep since Landon was dropped off around 5 a.m. each morning, but I managed. When I fed them breakfast, I usually fed one at a time. They both acted as if they were starved one morning, so I asked Peter to feed Leann. It shouldn't have been a big deal, but it was. She tried to grab the spoon, like babies that age typically do, and he was irritated. His irritation turned to anger and he snapped at her. I watched him closely. When I saw him raise his hand to slap her across the face, something inside me snapped.

"You might beat my ass right now, but so help me God if you hit her I will cut your throat in your sleep."

I could tell he was surprised I had the courage to say something, especially something so bold. He stepped around the table and stood in front of me. I didn't move. I expected him to hit me, but he just stood there staring at me. I meant what I said and was willing to take a beating to keep her safe. I would not back down from him. I stood tall and stared right back at him.

The look on his face told me he was shocked I didn't flinch. I always flinched when he moved too fast or raised his voice when he was within reach. He walked around me and went down the hallway to our bedroom. I was left with both kids and was safe for the moment. I stopped babysitting not long after that incident. I refused to put a child in danger that didn't have to be in the midst of it all.

I started sleeping on the couch when Peter was home, but he rarely stayed at the house. I picked him up from work and he would take me home. He stayed out all night until a few hours before he had to leave. He would come home and take a shower, and I would take him to work. That was how things were. We were separated but still lived in the same house. He wasn't going to move out, and I chose not to push the issue. As long as he left me and the baby alone, I wouldn't bother.

Over time, his attitude changed. I'm not sure what happened, but he stayed home more often. If I had to guess what changed, I would say whoever he had been seeing broke it off with him. He was nicer to me and was nicer to the baby. That is what mattered to me—he was nicer to Leann. He acted as if he really wanted to fix things, and we started sleeping in the same bed again. We were working things out, and it seemed to be going well for a little while.

After his anger reappeared, I pulled away from him. He apologized, and that was something he had not done in a long time. Peter decided he wanted to take a vacation in hopes it would relieve the tension and make things better at home. I figured it was worth a shot. I had been through much worse. At that point, I felt I had come so far and taken so much hoping to make things work with him that I shouldn't be so quick to walk away if he was trying.

We left to take our vacation a week before Leann's first birthday. My sister went with us, which meant I wouldn't be alone with him. Peter's father lived about four hours from us, and we didn't often see him. Paul Bennett had never seen the baby, and he lived along the way. It was a good time to let him meet his granddaughter. He fell in love with Leann the minute he saw her. Paul asked if we would stop by and pick him up on our way home. He wanted to stay with us for a while and spend time with his grandchildren. Paul was a wanderer and never sat still for long. Neither of us thought he would be there when we came back, so telling him we would pick him up after out trip was not a big deal.

The next week was filled with laughter and lots of fun. We enjoyed our vacation. We really did. There was no fighting, and I thought things were going to be okay. It was the first time in a long time I really believed we could make it work. The romance seemed to return, and I let my guard down. I had suffered, sacrificed, and forgiven so much. After all the blood, sweat, and tears I put into the relationship, it seemed stupid not to give it another chance.

When we headed home, we stopped by his father's house and were surprised to find him packed and ready to go. It was unexpected, but it would be good for the baby to get to know her grandfather. The first few days with our new house guest were tough, but we made it work.

Paul was rough around the edges. He drank heavily and tended to be loud and boisterous. Still, he adored Leann, and Leann loved him. She giggled nonstop, and I was willing to tolerate his annoying quirks if it made her happy.

I corrected him quite a few times in the first few weeks, but he willingly adjusted. He was so in love with the baby that I think he would have stood on his head in the corner if I asked. Peter still wanted little to do with Leann, and he had already returned to his old ways—hateful and agitated. Paul still annoyed me, but he began to behave better and was giving Leann the father figure she lacked.

Tension mounted, and Peter's father noticed his anger issues. He asked several times if it was normal or if it was because he was there. There was a long-standing issue between the two of them due to a lengthy estrangement. I shrugged and told him it was better than it usually was.

Peter became more and more comfortable showing out in front of his dad. My fear grew, and I walked on eggshells. His father noticed the change in my behavior when he was home and when he was gone. When he asked if everything was okay, I lied. I said things were pretty much like every other married couple. I knew what was going on was not normal, but I didn't trust Paul. If I told him how things really were and he was on Peter's side, I would surely take a beating. I kept my mouth shut, but the truth always comes out in the end.

One day before Peter was leaving for work, Leann was playing in the kitchen. She loved pulling the pots and pans out of the lower cabinet and banging them on the floor. When she pulled out the first pot, he reached over to smack her. My father-in-law snapped when he saw Peter intended to hit the baby.

"If you hit her, I will put you through the damn floor."

I knew right then he would keep Leann safe. I could endure whatever Peter had in store for me, but knowing Leann was safe took a huge weight off my shoulders. After we dropped Peter off at work, Paul hopped in the front seat before we left. When we pulled out of the parking lot, he turned down the radio.

"Can I ask you something?"

I knew what he was going to ask. "Sure."

"Is he always like that? Has he done that before?"

"Like what?"

"Has he hit either one of you before?"

I drew in a deep breath. He was waiting for an answer, but I said nothing.

"So he has. How long has this been going on?"

Again, I said nothing.

"The whole time?"

I let out a long sigh and nodded. He sat there for a few minutes before he spoke again.

"I never thought..." He paused, shaking his head and tapping his fingers on the dashboard. "He's no son of mine. That's not a man."

I was uncomfortable with the conversation. Paul was still pretty much a stranger, and he was Peter's father. I reached over and turned the radio up again. He turned it off, and I knew he wasn't going to let it go.

"Why haven't you left him? This ain't right."

I still didn't speak. I didn't know if I could trust him. There were very few people I discussed any of it with because Mary had poisoned most people against me. It didn't help me to say anything. Nobody believed it, and the minute he found out I said something he made me pay for it.

Paul was not going to let it go.

"I'm serious. This shit ain't right. He's not a man. A man doesn't hit women and babies. I'm not gonna stand for him hitting on the baby. I'm not gonna stand for him hitting on you. He should know better than that shit. Have you told Mary?"

I fought hard but couldn't hold back the tears. My vision was blurred and I pulled over to get myself together. Perhaps it was because I was so upset. Perhaps it was because I held everything in for so long. I'm not sure why I did it, but I spilled it all. The words tumbled out and I couldn't stop myself. When I finally stopped speaking, I clasped my hand over my mouth. What had I done? If he found out I told his father, it would send him over the edge.

"You can't say anything. You can't. If he finds out..."

He looked out the window and shook his head. "You're that scared of him." It wasn't a question. It was a statement. He knew it was true without having to ask. "I was gonna go home soon, but I think I might need to stay a little longer."

I rubbed the tears from my eyes with the palms of my hands and wiped them on my jeans. I put the car in first gear and pulled out. The trip home was a long one. I didn't know what to say and didn't know if this was going to cause me more trouble. I was kicking myself for saying anything because I was certain I would regret it.

The next few days passed without any problems.

Paul didn't say anything, and I was thankful. Everyone was pretty quiet. The only sounds in the house were the giggles of Leann and Paul. There was no real conversation, and I was grateful.

Over the weekend, Mary and Kenneth brought James out to see his grandfather. It was the first time Mary had seen her ex-husband in years, but the visit went well. Paul and Kenneth had common interests and had a nice conversation about classic cars. I was surprised by the uneventful reunion. There was one small thing that puzzled me.

"I don't know why Mary just burst out in song like that. That's new. Maybe she was nervous."

Paul shook his head. "There was only one thing I ever really liked about her—her voice."

Surely not, I thought. There was no way she had a thing for the man she described many times as something akin to the devil. No way. I put it out of my head until he received calls from her several times a day every single day. I thought it was odd but still didn't think much of it until they started having lunch together once or twice a week. After a few weeks of this, I smirked at him when the phone rang. "Bet it's for you," I said with a giggle.

It was. He talked to her for about an hour while Leann and I played in the front yard. Paul joined us after he got off the phone. Leann was kicking leaves around on the ground and giggling. He picked her up and spun her around a few times. She laughed hysterically and begged to be picked up again when he sat her down on the ground. He reached down and spun her around once more.

"She really doesn't think much of you."

I shook my head. I knew she didn't.

"You already knew?"

"I'm surprised you're just now hearing how awful I am."

He laughed. "She talks about you a lot, actually."

"All nice, I'm sure." I cut my eyes at him. "Mary loves telling people how wonderful her Laura is."

He shook his head and laughed. "I see that."

CHAPTER FOURTEEN

Paul made friends in a neighboring county. He worked in his friend's store and stayed at his home so he could go back and forth to the store. I stopped by and picked him up on Peter's way to work so he could spend time with Leann on the weekends. We developed a routine with their work schedules. As hectic as it seemed, it was simple. It was simple because Leann was happy. No matter how many miles I drove or hours I spent in the car getting different people to different places, she was happy.

Peter was behaving fairly well. I think he realized his father wouldn't tolerate physical abuse. The emotional abuse was ongoing, but even that had calmed down a bit. Our relationship was complicated, but we still had a relationship and had sex on a fairly regular basis. Since he had a vasectomy months earlier, birth control wasn't a concern. The thought of pregnancy didn't cross my mind when my period was late. He was supposed to be sterile. As soon as he realized I was late, he took the day off work and rushed to the store to buy a pregnancy test.

"There's no way I'm pregnant. It's impossible."

When two lines showed in the small windows, I collapsed on the bathroom floor. This would keep me chained to him. I had been working up the nerve to kick him out, but this would make it impossible. I sat on the bathroom floor, sobbing and shaking.

He helped me up and led me to the couch. Peter plopped down in the recliner. He leaned forward and started to speak, but a knock on the door stopped him. The timing couldn't have been worse. Paul and I liked to play cards, but we needed more than two people to make the game interesting. On Friday nights, two guys would stop by to play cards with Paul and me. I'd make coffee, and we would sit and play gin rummy or bullshit. Paul wasn't there, and only one of the guys showed up that night. I explained to him we weren't playing cards, and he left. As soon as he walked out the door, Peter started.

"Is he the father?"

I could not believe he was accusing me of cheating. I was with Peter, Paul, or Leann all the time. Peter was without a doubt the father of the baby. There was no other option, and I wished that was not true. It would have been an easy way to get rid of him. He was the father, and I was going to be stuck. He would have to accept he was not sterile and was the father, and I was going to have to accept it, too. We agreed not to tell anyone yet because we both needed time to process it.

I should have kept taking my birth control pills. I should have, but Peter insisted I quit taking them after his vasectomy. He decided making me stop taking the pill would allow him to catch me if I was cheating. I had no intention of cheating, so I agreed to throw them in the trash without protest. Now…now I would pay a heavy price for it.

Paul came back the next day. After we took Peter to work, I decided to drive around for a little while. Leann loved to ride in the car, and we often took rides in the country right before sunset. I would roll the windows down and open the sunroof to let the wind blow through her hair. She would try to sing along to whatever song was on the radio, and it made me happy. Moments like this made everything else melt away.

The empty fields provided a blank canvas devoid of trees and power lines, and the sun never failed to paint it with splashes of beautiful colors. Paul always paused and said, "Thank you, Lord."

Leann would echo him from the back seat: "Tank ew!"

These moments are what kept me going. These memories were the small bit of sunlight that lit up the darkest days. It was enough to carry me through. I can still hear the sound of Sultans of Swing by Dire Straits belting from the speakers as I argued with Paul about his choice of 'the best song ever.' I can still hear Leann trying to sing it from the backseat while we discussed who controlled the radio. I can still picture the pink and orange skies over one of the best hills on my chosen route. I can see Leann trying to share her sippy cup and hear her telling me I could have a drink of the 'chockit milk' I bought her when I stopped at the convenience store on the way. I can hear and see it all because these memories played over and over in my mind to help me cope during the worst of times.

How would I handle this situation? I glanced at Leann in the rearview mirror. If I had another baby with him, I would be chained to him longer. Paul wouldn't be there forever. He was working a lot and didn't come over as much. I was left alone with Peter more than I wanted to be, and there was no way I could protect Leann while I was pregnant. Never in my life had I considered abortion an option for me. Never. I always said I could never do it. I never wanted to consider it, but I feared the imminent disappearance of what was now my best friend, Paul, and a pregnancy would put Leann in danger. Paul saved both of us from plenty of beatings, but we would be on our own most of the time, even if he decided his move from his hometown was permanent and stayed in the neighboring county. Every time I looked at her, I thought about her future. If I wanted her to have a normal life without fear, I would have to get away from him.

I spent months gathering my strength to push him out of my life for good. If I gave up then, I would likely never work up the nerve or the ability to do it again. It seemed like a now or never situation, and I knew what option made the best sense. I made an appointment to have an abortion. I spent the next few days hating myself for choosing to get rid of one child to make it easier for another. I hated myself for even thinking about it, but I kept repeating in my head that it was what I needed to do. I told myself it was

THE LESSER OF TWO EVILS

necessary. The next week was spent with jags of crying and a heaping helping of self-loathing. There were many times when I considered canceling the appointment. It was still two weeks away. I still had time to decide.

Paul plopped down on the couch with Leann, and I broke down and told him I was pregnant. When I told him I was considering an abortion, he offered to help me get away from Peter. He told me he would assist financially until I had the baby and figured out how to manage on my own. I couldn't accept that offer. It was not his responsibility. I declined, and he told me the offer stood if I changed my mind because he would never stand back and watch his grandchildren suffer. It was a kind gesture from a great friend, but I couldn't accept.

My appointment was getting closer, and I tried figuring out how I could keep the baby and ditch him. What kind of person was I, choosing to abort a baby to save another? That made me an awful human being. Twice I had served my heart up on a silver platter to spare James from being hurt. Was I willing to sacrifice a child's life to spare Leann from being hurt? I waffled back and forth about it. Somehow, I would make it work. I didn't want to go through with the abortion and decided I wasn't going to do it. I knew having an abortion would be something I regretted my entire life. That was that. I was having a baby. I didn't know how I would manage, but I knew it was what I wanted.

The next time I spoke to Paul privately he told me

he had an interesting conversation with Mary.

"She knows you're pregnant. Peter told her."

I was annoyed. We said we would hold off on telling anyone. Of course, I had told Paul so I couldn't be terribly angry about it. I could, but it would be total hypocrisy on my part.

"I'm sure she had something nice to say."

He nodded. "Yep. She asked me what I thought about it and pointed out that Peter had a vasectomy a little while ago."

"I see. So, now she's saying the baby isn't his, right?"

"Yep."

"I would probably be better off if I let them believe it. Then I wouldn't have to deal with them if I could get him to leave."

He paused and shook his head. "You know that's not how it would go. You'd end up in court fighting over it, and you know how that would end. If they fought over it, they'd want to keep it and you'd be dealing with the same shit as James."

I knew he was right. If I made them go to court to determine paternity, once they found out it was Peter's baby they would fight for it as revenge. The purpose of choosing not to have an abortion was to keep the baby, not have them take it away. Now I was reconsidering my decision. No matter what I did, I was afraid it would end poorly. I decided to take my chances. In the next couple of weeks, I would need to figure out how to get him out of the picture and convince him it wasn't his baby. I had a lot of thinking to do.

A few days later, I started bleeding. It was heavy and kept getting worse. I was thankful Paul was there to watch Leann or I would have been alone trying to deal with her. I passed four very large clots—each around the size of a cantaloupe. The room started to spin and wave after wave of cramping hit me hard. I packed my underwear full of pads, but as soon as I stood up I had to change them again.

I managed to make my way down the hall.

"Paul? Paul, we have to pick up Peter and go to the emergency room."

I don't remember the ride, and I don't remember going in the hospital. Paul later told me I was talking gibberish the entire trip. I had gone into shock. Despite the blood loss, they did not admit me to the hospital. I had two different types of insurance. The two didn't play nicely with billing, and they didn't want to deal with it. They confirmed the baby was deceased and told me I would need to have a D&C. The doctor told me to see an obstetrician to schedule surgery but didn't bother to make a referral or recommendation. I was still feeling faint when they sent me out the door.

I felt stupid crying over the loss of a baby I considered aborting, but that's exactly what I did. Even though abortion was an option, I decided to keep it. I ran scenarios through my mind over and over trying to figure out how to make things work, and I almost had it figured out. The decision was ultimately made for me. I felt relieved and sad at the same time. I thought I had to be the most horrible person who ever lived.

After struggling to find an obstetrician that would deal with my insurance situation, I finally found a doctor who would perform a D&C. Almost two weeks after finding out my baby was dead, the last pieces of it were removed from my body. I was in terrible shape by then. I had dealt with heavy bleeding for so long that I was weak.

Paul helped with Leann for the next few days so I could rest and recover some of my strength. He had helped with her so much since the night of my emergency room visit. It shouldn't have been that way, but my father-in-law, not my husband, was the biggest help during my brief pregnancy and miscarriage.

The next month was rough, but I summoned the courage to tell Peter it was over and he needed to find a place to go. I took him out on the porch and told him while Leann and Paul played on the living room floor. I felt safer with Paul there, but I had not warned him.

Peter stormed into the house and looked at Paul. "Did you know about this?"

Paul was baffled. "About what?"

"She wants me gone. Did you know about this?"

Of course he knew I wanted to leave Peter. He encouraged me to leave him for Leann's sake. He told me many times it didn't help Leann for me to be beaten and broken. Paul warned me if she grew up around it she would think it was normal and might end up in the same situation when she grew up. He knew it would eventually happen, but he had no clue it was happening right then.

"She should." He was not a person that could be intimidated and said what was on his mind. "If you took care of your family like a real man, she wouldn't be leaving you."

"I pay all the bills here. They don't go without."

"There's a lot more to taking care of your family

than paying bills—like keeping your hands off them. She should have left you a long time ago, and that's your own fault."

Peter stared at me for a minute. I knew the look. He was disgusted with me and wanted to hurt me. It didn't matter that I wasn't alone. I was still afraid.

"I'll find a place to go, but it will take a little while."

"Fine."

He slowly shook his head back and forth and snarled his lip. "Nobody's gonna want you. You've got two kids, and you're worn out. Look at you. Guess you want to be alone for the rest of your life."

I watched him walk out the door and leave in the car. I was grateful he left, but I burst into tears the minute he was gone. Paul picked up Leann and sat her on the couch beside me.

"Those things he said…you know that's not true. There's nothing wrong with you."

"It's more than that. As soon as he gets the chance, he's likely going to kill me."

Paul scrunched up his face and stuck his tongue out at Leann. She giggled, and her big brown eyes sparkled. She climbed down and ran across the room to return to her pile of toys on the floor.

"Look, you're doing the right thing. You know you're doing the right thing. Look at Leann. She deserves better than this. You deserve better than this."

"I know. I'm just scared of what he's going to do."

He shook his head. "No reason to be scared. I'll stick around until he's gone. Then everything will be fine. Just promise me something, will ya?"

"What?"

"Don't keep me from seeing Leann."

"I would never do that. She loves you."

"I love her, too, and I want to be in her life."

"I promise I won't do that to you. No matter what happens with Peter, I promise I won't keep her away from you."

It was a huge weight off my shoulders, knowing I would have protection for at least a little while. Having some of the fear melt away made all the difference. I would be free, and this time I wasn't going to go back to him. This time I was going to start my own life.

CHAPTER FIFTEEN

Over the next few weeks, Peter stayed gone most of the time. I slept in my bed when he wasn't home and slept on the couch when he was. We lived separate lives, but he was still living in my house. I was growing tired of it, but I was giving him time to find a place of his own.

A friend of mine started hanging around the house with her boyfriend. I felt like a human being again and it showed. I dressed better. I looked better. I felt better. When her boyfriend brought one of his friends to my house, we hit it off and started talking. Within a few weeks, we were dating. It wasn't wrong and wasn't cheating. Peter still lived in my house, but I was separated and waiting for him to leave.

A couple of months passed, and Peter had not left.

He continued mentally abusing me and taunting me with threats of physical abuse, but I was stronger. The encouragement of my father-in-law and best friend gave me strength, and my new relationship gave me hope. The two combined were enough to motivate me to take action. I had moved on and there was no place for him in my life. Peter had to go.

Experience taught me to take precautions. I knew the tactics Peter and Mary used to keep me under their control, and I was not taking chances. My mother picked up Leann to keep him from trying to take her when he left. I was prepared for whatever happened. He might beat me. He might kill me. One way or another, everything would end.

I sat on the couch and waited for him to return. He arrived with a friend of his, and the phone rang as soon as he entered the door. I could tell by the look in his eyes he was livid. Words cannot describe how angry he appeared. When he hung up the phone and asked his friend to leave, I braced for the worst. I thought he was going to take my life, but I knew my daughter would be safe no matter what he did to me. Whatever happened was worth the price I would pay.

"Is this shit true?"

I didn't say anything. I wasn't sure how much he knew, so I didn't know how to respond.

"That was mom, and your grandmother called her. Your sister told her I was moving out today and she's moving in as soon as I leave."

Damn. I lost control of the situation before I had a chance to speak.

Thanks, sis. Your big mouth might be what pushes him over the edge and gets me killed.

My mother asked if I would let my pregnant sister,

who was homeless, move in with me once he was gone. I agreed but warned them to keep it quiet. Apparently, mom told her, she immediately told my grandmother, and my grandmother told Peter's mother. Now that he learned about all the plans over the phone, he was livid.

I found myself trying to sink into the couch cushions the same way I did when my father held a gun to my head. Fear surged through my body, and I wasn't sure I could find my voice. I had to say it. The decision had been made.

"Yes." My voice trembled when I said it. I braced for the worst.

"Where is Leann?"

"At my mom's house." I knew then I did the right thing in choosing to send her away while I took care of this.

He swung his fist through the air, but he was not aiming at me. His reaction scared me even more. It was quiet for a few minutes, and I watched him shake and clinch his fists over and over. He wanted to hit me. It was clear he wanted to hurt me, but he didn't. I wasn't sure why.

Peter picked up the phone and called his friend to help him move some furniture. We had a second living room suite, and I was able to keep one. The bed was given to me by my mother, so he couldn't take it. He took the kitchen table, the entertainment center and television, and various other pieces throughout the house. I was left with the necessities: a refrigerator, stove, washer and dryer, and beds. I had what I needed to take care of Leann, and that was all that mattered.

When he drove away, I called my mother. "He's

gone. No, I'm okay. Surprisingly, I'm okay. Just shaken up."

I hung up the phone and sat there in silence. It was over. It was finally over for good. I wept. Years of pain and fear had ended, and it was a sobering moment. This was what I wanted, and I made sure I wouldn't go back. I replaced him with a new romantic interest. Some people won't agree with that part of my journey, and that's okay. It was one of several things I needed to keep me from going back to him. I also had roommates moving in to keep me from letting him come back. The bedroom became my sister and brother-in-law's room so I felt like I wasn't in charge of the house. This helped me feel like I couldn't allow him to come back. These were all things I needed to do to ensure I didn't give in to him in a moment of weakness or fear.

It wasn't easy. I was left without a vehicle, and my sister and brother-in-law didn't have one, either. My brother-in-law took a job with a construction company close to the house. Transportation wasn't a problem for him. I got a job as a housekeeper at a hotel. My shift started at 9 a.m. each morning, and I worked until my assigned rooms were completed.

The hotel was about 8 miles from my home. The only option I had was to ride to town with my neighbors. They went to work at 5 a.m., and I sat in the motel's office for almost four hours every morning while I waited for my shift to start. My shift ended when my work was done, and I never knew when that would be. Sometimes my father would pick me up and take me home. Sometimes I would walk to my grandmother's house and my grandfather or father would drive me home. There were a couple of times when I walked all the way home. No matter how difficult it was, I did it. I was going to keep doing it because I was determined I was going to make it.

I did everything I could at the time, but I barely covered my half of the bills. My mother bought everything Leann needed. Peter gave me $100 a couple of weeks after I kicked him out of the house, but that was the only time he offered to help support her.

My father-in-law stopped by one afternoon to spend time with the baby. We sat on the ground while she played in the front yard. He offered to help financially, but I declined. I was not his responsibility, and I told him that.

"What if I want you to be? What if I want to take care of you and Leann?"

"You shouldn't. She's not your responsibility. She's Peter's. I'm certainly not your responsibility. I couldn't let you do that."

He reached over and grabbed my hand and cradled it in his. "You don't understand. I love you and want to make sure you're okay."

I smiled. He was my best friend and had already done so much for me. "I love you, too, but you shouldn't have to take care of us. I don't want you to do that. You've already done so much more than you know. I would still be stuck under his thumb without your help."

"No, you don't understand. I love you."

Oh.

How did this happen? I loved Paul so much, but

not in a romantic way. He changed my life in a way I could never repay, and I would always be grateful. I wanted us to be lifelong friends, but any type of relationship aside from friendship was out of the question. This was completely unexpected, and I didn't know how to react.

"Paul, we can't do that. I...I'll never claim I'm an angel. I'm not, but there are lines I won't cross. That's one."

"After everything he's done to you, you shouldn't be worried about his feelings."

"It's not his feelings I'm worried about."

He was frustrated. "Then what? What is it? Why are you worried about what people think?"

I let out a long sigh. I didn't want to have this conversation with him. I never wanted things to go this way. I didn't.

"Paul, we're friends. You're my best friend, and we'll always be friends. I want you around and want you to be a big part of Leann's life. I want you to be part of my life—but not like that. You know I love you, but not like that."

He stood up and dusted off his pants. "I better get back and take care of things around the house."

"Don't go. I don't want it to be like that."

He turned away from me. He turned away, and I knew. Our friendship was over. I didn't want it to be, but he didn't want to be just friends.

"I gotta go." He kissed Leann on the forehead and left.

That conversation with Paul was the last real conversation I had with him, and it will play over and over in my head until the day I die. If he hadn't helped me and given me the courage I needed, I'm not sure I would have escaped my former life. Paul was upset I didn't share his feelings, and he went back to his hometown. I won't say he was angry with me. I believe his heart was broken. The once-tough and rugged man who could handle his own had been softened by his granddaughter and me. He was more of a pacifist than a fighter when he returned home, thanks to my grooming. It was this that caused him to shy away from a fight that resulted in his murder. I will carry that guilt forever. I changed him, then I broke his heart. He went home and would never return. Leann would not grow up knowing the love he had for her, and my friend truly was gone. The man who saved me was killed because he became the friend I needed to save me. There is a hole in my heart and a guilt that will always nag at me.

CHAPTER SIXTEEN

I was drowning, but I wasn't living in fear. It was worth it. It was worth every struggle I had, and there were plenty. Life was good no matter how much I struggled…until it wasn't.

I was flat broke and barely surviving. Leann and I certainly couldn't have survived on our own. Paying bills took every dime I made, and I didn't have enough money to buy what my daughter needed. My mother paid for her necessities. Buying a car to search for a better job was out of the question, and hiring a lawyer was definitely out of the question.

The thing about divorce is if one person can't afford an attorney, the person with an attorney is awarded whatever they ask for in court. I contacted legal aid in hopes of getting help with a lawyer. I was informed the only way they would provide an attorney was if he asked for sole custody with no visitation. That wasn't the case. Without an attorney of my own, Peter received custody of Leann. My heart was absolutely broken. I was ripped to shreds and didn't know how to make things better.

I moved out of my house and moved in with my then-boyfriend. Peter learned a few tricks through his mother's antics with James, and he put his knowledge to use. He knew he could use my daughter to lead me around by the nose, and he did. Peter would allow me to see my daughter if I went to his house and had sex with him. I couldn't live without seeing my daughter, so that's exactly what I did many, many times.

There isn't much I wouldn't have done to be with her, even if just for a little while. I did the same for James. Repeatedly sacrificing my body and my sanity for my children is not something I will ever regret. Anyone who believes they would refuse his proposal has never been placed in that situation. You would, without hesitation. I allowed him to abuse my body in many ways to see James. This was no different. It was just more abuse, and I had endured much worse over the years.

When Paul was injured, we did not find out about it for several weeks. As soon as I learned he was in the hospital, I chose to make the long trip. He was in a hospital on the other side of the state, and it meant I had to ride in a car alone with Peter for hours. It didn't matter. Paul was in serious condition, and I had to see him.

His face lit up when he saw me. Peter stepped out to speak to the doctor, and I stayed in the room with him.

"Fight hard. As soon as we're able to take you home, I'll come back and take care of you. I'll take care of you for the rest of your life. I promise."

He was my best friend, and I meant it. Paul had done so much for me. I owed it to him, no matter the cost. He would have done it for me. He had indeed offered to do it for me.

Paul had a tracheotomy and was unable to speak, but he shook his head when I told him I would go back to take care of him. He tried speaking, but couldn't make a sound. I read his lips and saw what he was trying to say: "No. Leann."

I knew what he meant. He didn't want me to go back because of her. He didn't want me to put her back in that situation. Paul did not know Peter had custody of her, and I would not tell him. Not then. He gently shook his head every time I told him I would take care of him. He tried speaking again: "I love you."

Those were the last words he tried to say to me.

"I love you, too. Leann loves you. You have to get better so you can come home. We'll take care of you."

He gently shook his head and squeezed my hand.

Peter returned to the room and told me it was time to leave. We arrived long after visiting hours were over. The nursing staff let us in when they learned we just found out what happened and traveled a long way to see him. Paul was drifting off to sleep when I closed the door. That was the last time I saw him.

I wept when I found out he passed away. I was not told until after he was buried. Missing the funeral meant I was not allowed to grieve properly and had no closure. Guilt still eats at me. I made him soft, then I broke his heart. He went home, heartbroken, and was murdered. Peter said Paul told his brother he hated me and I was nothing but a whore. My guilt over what happened to him led me to believe he could have been angry enough he hated me. I now know it's not true, but I believed it for a long time. My heart was broken when Paul died. The friend who pushed me and helped me make the most important changes ever made in my life was gone.

Paul had placed a box underneath the bed in Leann's room. He told me he wanted her to have it and not to let Peter know it was there. It contained photos of him during his younger days and various things that were meaningful to him. There was only one photo of him and Leann, taken while they played in the front yard. I removed it from her photo album and gave the box and the photo to Peter. It was the only recent photo of him. I asked for her photo to be returned, but he kept it. Leann never saw the photo of the two of them.

She grew up knowing how he adored her, but she was never able to see what he looked like or see a photo of the two of them together. I regret giving him any of it. Leann should have had it like Paul wanted. She asked Peter for the photo of her and Paul many times over the years. He has not even shown her the photo.

During the time he was gone tending to his father's affairs after his death, he let my mother keep Leann. I was thrilled I would be able to see her without paying a price. Right after he dropped her off at mom's house, it became apparent she was very ill and needed to be taken to the hospital. She was weak and sick.

After his examination, the doctor stated she was

suffering from malnutrition. Peter had either forgotten to feed her or simply chose not to feed her. He forgot to feed his two-year-old child. How do you forget to feed a child? The answer lies in the other thing the doctor discovered: Leann had methamphetamine in her system. He forgot to feed her because he was too busy smoking crystal methamphetamine. Peter was doing hard drugs, and he was doing them close enough to her that it was in her system. She was given intravenous fluids and sent home. Leann spent the next year drinking supplemental nutrition drinks every day and taking vitamin supplements to build up her immune system.

While Peter was gone, we did what they taught us to do. We went to the judge, and my mother got emergency temporary custody. I told the judge I felt that was where she needed to be at the time to keep her safe from him. I was living with a man, unmarried, and that was enough for him to take me to court and petition for custody again. I still could not afford an attorney, so it would be impossible for me to fight. No matter how much he argued with my mother, I knew he was unable to take Leann from her. I was able to see her whenever I wanted, and she was safe. It was a temporary solution to a major problem.

Yet again, I made a tough decision to protect a child. It was necessary, and I would do it again without hesitation. My main objective was always to keep my children safe. I made many tough decisions over the years to protect them, and I regret none. They grew up with limited exposure to the dark, abusive side of Peter. That was what mattered. Of course, it wasn't that simple. It never was. Our fight did not end there.

CHAPTER SEVENTEEN

I will never claim to be an angel. I battled depression after they took my child and smoked pot on a fairly regular basis. Dealing with the separation after my first divorce, I was promiscuous and smoked pot off and on again. I drank and was all over the place. Nobody would say I was a good girl during any of that—not even me. I made plenty of mistakes and bad decisions over the years. Still, I am not ashamed of anything. I am not proud of it, but I'm not ashamed of what I did while coping with different issues. I survived. Despite the many times I was suicidal, I survived. That is what matters. I survived it all. It was part of my journey, and it all came together to shape me into who I am today.

My mistakes continued. I married my boyfriend

after I miscarried his child. Something was amiss in our relationship, but I didn't realize it until it was too late to walk away with ease. Warning signs of Robert's temper appeared before the ink was dry on our marriage certificate. Peter sent a dozen roses to my grandmother's house to stir up trouble. He continued doing everything he could to make me miserable. My grandmother said she was allergic, and the flowers had to go. They were beautiful, and I thought it a shame to throw them out. I tossed the card and took them home. Robert did not understand what was happening and didn't believe someone would do such things simply out of spite. He threw them at me.

Regardless of how things were, I felt it was probably the best I could do. As much strength as it took to leave Peter, I was still weak and broken. I was still grieving losing custody of Leann and Paul's death when I agreed to marry him. It was me surrendering to what I felt I deserved. It was all wrong, and I realized it not long after we were married. I left him a few weeks into our marriage but went back after he begged me to give it another chance.

Going back was the best thing I ever did, no matter how anyone else feels about what happened. People say everything happens for a reason, but you rarely find a legitimate reason for past events. There was most certainly a reason why it worked out as it did. I just didn't know yet.

My marriage was a total sham. Robert wanted little to do with me in any sense. I was a possession—a trophy. I don't think he ever wanted anything other than to own me. He had been caught talking to an ex-girlfriend before we were married, but I forgave him and let it go. We were in the same house every day but rarely spoke to each other in a meaningful way. It was awkward, to say the least.

Robert's cousin came to stay with us while he was home. John was a truck driver and traveled to various states. He was only going to be home for a couple of weeks and wanted to hang out with Robert while he was home. I was leery of his extended visit, but I agreed. John was loud and obnoxious, and I confess I hated him the first few days. He aggravated me to no end, until he didn't.

John didn't know his way around the county, and this was long before GPS was a big thing. He asked Robert to ride with him and show him where things were. When John wanted to go places, he began refusing to take him. Robert didn't ask me to drive his cousin wherever he wanted to go. He told me to do it. While we were out, we talked. My husband never talked to me, so I finally had someone to have a conversation with every day.

Over the course of our conversations, I told him how aggravated I was that Robert ignored me all the time. John informed me his cousin said he made a mistake marrying me. I already knew it was a mistake. Knowing he felt the same way told me everything I needed to know about our relationship. There was no real relationship. He didn't love me, and I didn't love him.

Robert kept pushing John and me together. After a week, I looked forward to it. He actually talked to me, and that was something I lacked. The first time he met Leann, I realized I was starting to like him in more than a friendly way. He sat on the floor and talked to her. Nobody else existed. He completely ignored everyone, including me, while she showed him all her toys. That was something no man had done since her grandfather lived with us. I admit I had a huge crush from that moment on, and I am not ashamed of it in the least.

John and I spent a great deal of time together before he left for his next job, and we were both sad when he prepared to leave. We spoke on the phone every day while he was gone, and we were both counting the days until he returned. The separations became too much for him. He quit before the next trip and found a job nearby so he wouldn't have to leave me. It was nice to have him around every day.

I worked as a tax preparer. My assignment was a booth in a department store, and I worked alone. Peter found out where I worked and showed up strung out, making me extremely uncomfortable. He was agitated, and I knew it. John called while he was there, and I was cryptic during our conversation. He realized Peter was there harassing me and rushed out the door. As soon as I hung up the phone, I told Peter that John was on his way to bring me lunch. He left before he arrived. John rushed to my rescue, and that was a lot more than my husband had ever done for me. I knew there was much more to this. Right then, I knew he cared about me, too.

Just a few weeks later, I told my husband I was in love with someone else and was leaving him. Robert grilled me to find out who it was, but I refused to tell him. John was still living in the house, and I didn't want things to get ugly. I told Robert I had someone coming to help me get my things. He left to give me time to pack up and move out of his house. His mother called John and asked him to make sure I didn't take anything that didn't belong to me. They didn't know. They had no clue, but they should have.

Peter found out we were a couple once we moved in together. He saw John at a gas station once and sneered at him, "You know I could get that any time I want. We've got two kids together. I'll always be able to hit that."

He was still obsessed with me, but I felt safe as long as John was around. I knew he wouldn't let anything happen to me. As long as he was close, I knew everything would be okay.

John and I dated for less than three months when he asked me to marry him. I was head over heels in love by that time, and so was Leann. I said yes without hesitation. We talked about having a child of our own and found out we were expecting just two months later. John found a great job, and we moved into a nice house. Leann moved in, and James came to stay with us from time to time. Life was great. It all happened so fast, and it was like a fairy tale. Never in my life had I dreamed things could be so perfect. Nothing is ever perfect, of course.

I developed placenta previa around sixteen weeks and was placed on bed rest for most of my pregnancy. John took care of Leann and me the entire time. He would place a bowl and a spoon on the table each morning and put a plastic bag filled with cereal inside it. He poured milk into a small cup and placed it on the refrigerator shelf for Leann's breakfast. She was three, and she was great throughout it all. She got up each morning and emptied her cereal into her bowl and poured the milk over it. After she finished her breakfast, she would turn on the television and sit on the couch. When I heard the TV, I would get up and make my way to the living room. We sat there together all day. She would get whatever John made us for lunch out of the fridge later on, and we just laid around all day. He loved us and took care of us. It was what Leann deserved, and over time I realized I deserved him, too.

I didn't have any interest in Peter being around Leann, but John did not have the history I had with him. It was easier for him, and he was a good man. He tried hard to get Peter to have some sort of relationship with her. When John found out Peter worked at a convenience store, he took her to see him at work. He stopped in on a regular basis, buying Leann chips or candy so she had a moment to say hello. After a couple of weeks of it, Peter quit his job. No matter how much John tried, Peter pulled away from her. He didn't want her. He didn't want either child. He just wanted me—not because he loved me, but because he wanted to own me.

John kept trying, and Peter kept avoiding Leann. She was at an age where she paid attention to everything. Peter had nothing to do with her, but John was there all the time. Other kids had men they called daddy. Peter wasn't there. John was. Leann chose to call John daddy. She wasn't told to call him that, but we didn't stop her. He became her daddy. He chose to be her dad, and Leann chose him to be her dad. Peter has been annoyed by it for years, but he left a vacant position and Leann filled it with John. She was so young when he came into our lives that she does not remember life before he was part of it. For her, he has been daddy all her life, and he has put

THE LESSER OF TWO EVILS

Peter in his place many times over the years when he did something to upset her.

Whenever Peter had a new girlfriend, he wanted to see Leann so he could show her off like some sort of show pony. He wanted to brag about his beautiful, smart, and well-mannered daughter, but he had nothing to do with how wonderful she was. He had some really nice girlfriends, and we trusted them with Leann. We allowed Leann to visit when he had a girlfriend because we trusted the girlfriends to take care of her. They did. She was safer with all of them than she ever was with her father.

One particular woman, Janet, had a little boy close to her age. The two of them got along very well, and she adored Leann. She even put up a special pink Christmas tree just for her. Peter asked to keep Leann over the weekend. He was staying with Janet, and we trusted her. She called us late Saturday night and told us Peter disappeared more than 24 hours earlier. My first concern was he had Leann with him. She assured me she was still at her house. He dropped Leann off with her right after he picked her up and left. John told her we would be right over to pick her up, but she asked for Leann to stay and play with her son. We let her spend the night and went to pick her up the next day. She would have made a great stepmother to Leann, but Peter couldn't straighten up to keep a decent woman.

After the birth of our son, Jacob Tyler, we moved to a bigger house. Peter had a new girlfriend, Paula. She was a sweet girl. Paula was pregnant when they met, and he made her many promises. She fell in love with Leann, and I trusted her. She would go stay with them some weekends. When they came to pick her up,

Paula would often sit and play cards with us and chat before they left. I really liked her, but I worried about the safety of her and her baby. I knew how he treated his own child. How would he treat someone else's baby? She didn't deserve it. She was a nice girl.

Peter and Paula came over to pick up Leann on a Friday afternoon, and Peter wanted to speak in private. I was still very much afraid of him because I knew the real Peter. I stood just outside the door where I was in plain view. There was a stick nearby, and he picked it up off the ground. His voice was slightly raised, and he waved it around near my head. John and our friend noticed it and kept a close eye on the situation. Their reaction was noted by Paula. I'm fairly certain that was when she started noticing his odd behaviors.

Leann stayed with them the weekend before Easter. When we went to pick her up, Peter was gone. Paula bought her a chocolate Easter bunny, and Peter bought nothing for her. She didn't deserve what he would end up doing to her, so I told her what he had done to his daughter and me. I told her I worried that if he did his child the way he did he would be cruel to her child. No child deserves it, but her baby had no connection to him and could be spared his wrath. She left him shortly after that. I hated she was gone because I really liked her, but because I liked her I was glad she left him.

When Peter moved to Colorado, the tension eased. I was safe when he was gone, and I enjoyed the time I didn't have to look over my shoulder. It didn't last long. He moved back after I started working part-time in a grocery store deli. Once he found out I worked there, he called the store many times during my shift. I was the only person in the deli, so I had no choice but to answer the phone. Every time I hung up, he would call right back. He did it over and over until I was sure I would get fired. I talked to the owner about the issue. Thankfully, he understood the situation.

Peter decided to show up at the store, and I was shaken by his appearance at my job. He still wanted me, so I was not safe. His main intention was to try to cause trouble in my marriage and to let me know he could always get to me no matter where I was. I knew this because I knew him. I knew the games he played, and I was afraid.

I strongly considered quitting my job the first time he showed up, but John agreed to randomly show up at the store during my shift. I warned Peter he would stop in randomly to make sure he left me alone. The owner instructed me to call his office immediately if I had any problems and assured me he would make sure it was handled until police arrived. Everyone around me worked to keep me safe, and I was grateful.

When I found out I was pregnant with my fourth child, I quit immediately. I had five miscarriages in the past and didn't want to take any chances. It was a lot less stressful knowing I didn't have to worry about him calling me or showing up at my job.

Peter moved back to Colorado and was back and forth between states. When he came home, he sent me a registered letter asking to see Leann. I ignored it. He was using meth again, and I knew it. There was no way I was going to allow her to be around him after what he did to her in the past. He was angry and threatened to have me arrested for contempt of court.

My pregnancy was considered high risk due to my previous miscarriages. I had been told the baby had choroid plexus cysts on her brain and might have Down Syndrome. To say it was a stressful time would be an understatement of epic proportions. I did not need the additional worries.

"Fine. Have me arrested if you want."

Peter was so angered by my refusal and flippant response that he threatened to kidnap Leann, telling me I would never see her again. I spoke to a friend in law enforcement and was informed it was considered a civil matter. If he took her, I would have to take him to court and have a judge settle it. Once it went to court, they had problems enforcing and resolving these issues across state lines and it could take a long time to get her back.

Leann was in kindergarten, and we took every precaution to keep him from getting to her. Her school was informed of the situation. A very short list of people could pick her up—me, John, my mother, and my stepfather. We told her teacher my stepfather would pick her up after school one day when I had a doctor's appointment, and the teacher demanded he show identification before they let her come out of the building. I felt very comfortable with how they worked to ensure her safety at school.

John and I made plans to keep her safe at all costs. We decided if officers came to arrest me for contempt, John would take Leann somewhere Peter couldn't find her until I was out of jail. It would keep him from taking her while I was gone. She would not be exposed to meth again. She was a little older, and we did not want her around crack heads and crack houses. I heard horror stories about what some of them did to little girls. I did not want her exposed to meth, anyone on meth, or a father who threatened to kidnap her.

When he realized he would have to come back for a court date, he decided to drop the contempt of court issue. He left, and life was nice again. Leann's life was nice again. Peter's appearances and disappearances weren't good for her. He only wanted to show her off when he found someone new or to appease his mother's desire to keep up appearances. He didn't care about Leann. He cared about looking like a good father to impress new girls. He cared about doing what his mother wanted. They both cared about finding a way to use Leann to make me miserable like they used James.

CHAPTER EIGHTEEN

Mary wanted to make things hard for me. James started visiting us, and his desire to visit annoyed her. He enjoyed playing video games with Leann and his younger brother, Jacob, at our house and wanted to come out frequently to play. She was bothered by that, so she bought him a brand-new game system of his own. He stopped wanting to come out as often. It hurt me, and she knew it. She couldn't have James wanting to actually be around me, and she took action each time it happened over the years.

We bought a house right before our youngest child was born. When Chelsea Marie was about a year old, we bought a small above ground swimming pool. James wanted to come out often to swim with Leann, Jacob, and Chelsea. She bought him a bigger pool to keep him home. Every time he wanted to visit, Mary bought him something new. The last big purchase she made for him was a four-wheeler. His visits became further and further apart, and he started getting in trouble.

She allowed him to run around on his four-wheeler at all hours of the night. He broke his arm when he had a wreck while making a 2 a.m. trip to a 24-hour convenience store on the highway. James was arrested twice in one day when he was 14 years old. He was arrested for assault, and once he was released, he was arrested again for vandalism of city property. He was placed on house arrest and only allowed to leave the house with me or one of his grandparents. He had to be home before sundown or he was in violation. When he was 17, he was arrested for simple possession and placed on state probation.

Mary's response to his arrest for possession of marijuana was nonchalant. "He's 17. What can I do?"

She could have done the job she went to such great lengths to secure—the job of a parent. James didn't work, so she gave him money. She bought him the truck he ran around in and paid to keep gas in it. The money and truck should have been gone. I would have grounded him to the house, but she had no idea how to do anything but let him run wild and throw money at him. She did the same thing with Peter, which was why he behaved the way he did, doing as he pleased and letting her pick up the tab for everything. Mary chose to be his friend rather than act as a parent, and it was not the first time she made that mistake.

Mary didn't stop until she won the battle with James. She purposely poisoned him until our relationship could not be repaired, going as far as concocting outlandish stories and forging letters to drive the final nail in the coffin. The forgeries were something new thrown at me during the last argument I had with Peter.

At that moment, I gave up and accepted it all. He belonged to Mary, and he was one of them. She clipped his wings and emotionally enslaved him the same way she enslaved Peter. I was naive to think he would figure out the truth when he grew up and became a man. Mary made sure to work her magic and spin a web of lies to keep him entangled with her convincing words. How was he to believe lies he was told his entire life were untrue? It wasn't his fault. He simply lived what he learned. He was lost, and all I could do was hope he didn't choose the same paths as Peter.

I have come to terms with what happened in my life because I've had no choice. Leann knows the truth because she lived it. She was kept safe throughout her childhood. She was never punched by Peter like James was. She didn't have to deal with frequent angry outbursts like James did. Leann wasn't exposed to his meth addiction as frequently as he was, and she had a more stable home life. She grew up in a home with a loving family who provided structure, support, guidance, and appropriate discipline.

James didn't have the support and encouragement she had. Nobody urged him to do more than exist. He was not told he could be more than what they were. He learned what he lived and then lived what he learned. He learned to hate, and he learned to hate me. I can't change that any more than I could change Peter. How I wish I could have provided James with what Leann had growing up, but Mary didn't want him to have a real relationship with me, his stepfather, or his siblings.

Peter and many others were molded by Mary to be her minions, but they failed to realize what she had done to them. They were also her victims. They couldn't see she clipped their wings and grounded them. She employed them to do her bidding, but they were blind to it. They were dependent on her in many ways. They craved her approval because they were trained and enslaved by her just as I was by Peter. The only difference was she didn't beat them. She had a way of speaking to them that kept them in line by suggesting they would lose her favor. They were so accustomed to her narcissistic ways that they understood the hierarchy of their relationships—obey me as your master, and I will show you love. Mary ruined their relationships with others and ostracized them from many people who could have greatly enriched their lives.

If someone wishes to know why Peter was the way he was, one has to look no further than his mother. He took her abusive behavior a step further by adding physical abuse to emotional abuse, but make no mistake. He mimicked behavior he learned from Mary. He was taught to be who he was.

When Peter was older and more difficult to control, she used a financial leash. He remained financially dependent upon her throughout his life. He managed on his own for brief periods of time, but he always ended up back at her house, begging for money.

Peter was chronically unemployed for years and maintained a crystal meth addiction. Mary handed him money, feeding his addiction and effectively condoning his behavior through financial support of his habit. Despite his addiction and refusal to work, she welcomed him back home as long as he did her bidding. His tasks have included harassing Leann for refusing to fall in line and kiss the ring of the demented matriarch.

They tried forcing her to assimilate into their way of thinking by ostracism. These tactics never worked on her because she wasn't bothered by their lack of affection. She never lacked affection at home. She had a full family life with love and affection—love without conditions or caveats. That was something Peter and James did not experience, and it is the primary reason why they craved her approval and Leann did not.

Peter tries the same tricks his mother used on him to decide whether or not he shows Leann affection. He asks her for favors, including money. He has even asked her to do things that could result in physical harm, and Mary knew. Leann won't obey him, and he has little use for someone who won't obey. Peter doesn't realize that when she chose a daddy after he vacated the position, it made all the difference in her life. She doesn't need him, and he can't control her. It always bothered him.

I lived my life in fear, hiding away in my home and refusing to leave unaccompanied. His words echoed in my head, and it affected me many ways over the years. I am no longer afraid, and I never will be again. When an incident arose involving my grandchildren, I snapped once more. My fear subsided when I felt the renewed strength flowing through my veins as it did once before. That was the end of the last bit of control he had over me—fear.

Many times I've wondered how different things would be if Mary was merely a quiet librarian who was genuinely kind and loving. I am certain there would be many differences, but grieving over the past is pointless.

I have a good life. I love, and I am loved. Peter has not ruined my life, but his attempts have derailed his own. He is alone, battling addiction, and dependent upon his mother. He suffers because of the choices he has made and the choices Mary made for him.

Knowing the life Peter has led, mistakes he has made, and the significant chance he will be alone in his last days, if I could say one last thing to Peter, it would be this: In the words of my dear friend Paul, "Sorry about your luck, but it's not my problem."

CHAPTER NINETEEN

Twenty years after I left for the last time, I finally truly escaped. I am no longer afraid, and I don't live my life fearing what he might do to me. I no longer care what he or his mother have to say about me or the rumors they spread in an attempt to discredit me. I just don't care. I'm free. I'm finally free.

If you are still trying to find a way out, know that you will find a way and escape. If you are still fighting to get back on your feet after escaping, know you will be okay and it will get better. If you are still recovering, know that it will happen. Don't give up the fight.

No matter what stage you are in at the moment, know that you are strong, you are worthy of happiness, your scars do not define you, and it was never your fault.

I'm rooting for you. I'm thinking of you and your struggles. I know you can do this. I know you can, and I know because I did it.

You are not alone.

ABOUT THE AUTHOR

Amy Pilkington was born and raised in a small town in Tennessee. The rural town is so small cows outnumber people. She still lives in that same little county but wants to be a beach bum when she grows up. Pilkington is married to a great guy and has four wonderful children, two spoiled dogs, a beautiful granddaughter, and a handsome grandson.

This introverted writer has a broad range of interests and a tendency to bore quickly, which explains her varied works in multiple genres. Regardless, her works tend to delight readers and keep them coming back for more. Her series devoted to the pinup girls of World War II continues to attract fans thirsty for a glimpse into the lives of starlets who lit up the silver screen during the war. She intends to continue feeding her fans a wide array of reading material.

Pilkington enjoys reading, photography, travel, and a tall glass of sweet tea. She also likes camping, but she's not one to rough it. Her thoughtful husband takes her into the wilderness in their fifth-wheel trailer so she can have all the comforts of home while watching wildlife.

Connect

Follow Amy Pilkington on social media to learn more about her other books and keep up with her latest projects.

Facebook: PilkingtonPublishing

Twitter: __amypilkington

Instagram: amyp0807

Made in the
USA
Lexington, KY